"..."
I was sure ... ...
mate.

"You're really into this astrology stuff, aren't you?" Dean countered. His smoky gray eyes gazed into mine.

I nodded. "You're stalling. Just tell me your sign."

"Okay, okay. If it's so important to you. I'm a Gemini."

I couldn't believe it. Dean Smith, the love of my life, was a . . . Gemini. Completely the wrong astrological sign.

In the past, I had been badly hurt by a two-faced, back-stabbing Gemini. Since then, I'd promised myself that I would never let that happen again.

Now there was only one choice. I had to break up with Dean. . . .

Don't miss any of the books in *Love Stories*
—the romantic series from Bantam Books!

Together Forever

Cameron Dokey

BANTAM BOOKS
NEW YORK · TORONTO · LONDON · SYDNEY · AUCKLAND

RL 6, age 12 and up

TOGETHER FOREVER
A Bantam Book / February 1997

Produced by Daniel Weiss Associates, Inc.
33 West 17th Street
New York, NY 10011.
Cover photography by Michael Segal.

ISBN: 0-553-57046-3

Published simultaneously in the United States and Canada

Bantam Books are published by Bantam Books, a division of Bantam
Doubleday Dell Publishing Group, Inc. Its trademark, consisting of the
words "Bantam Books" and the portrayal of a rooster, is Registered in
U.S. Patent and Trademark Office and in other countries. Marca
Registrada. Bantam Books, 1540 Broadway, New York, New York 10036.

PRINTED IN THE UNITED STATES OF AMERICA

OPM   0 9 8 7 6 5 4 3 2 1

To astrology lovers everywhere

One

NATALIE

Scorpio (Oct. 23–Nov. 21)
Stop dwelling in the past and look toward tomorrow.
Your reward could be new love. But old habits die hard,
particularly where your heart is concerned. Taurus individual will play healing role.

"I DON'T KNOW," I said, staring at my reflection
in the full-length mirror. "I think this dress is
too far out." I pivoted so that my best friend, Jayne
Engerman, could get a full view of me. "What do
you think?"

"Natalie Taylor, you're a prude!" Jayne exclaimed. "What's so far out about wearing red on
Valentine's Day?"

Jayne and I were in a dressing room in
Kleinfeld's, one of the most popular department
stores in Seattle. We'd been crowded into the tiny,
mirrored cubicle for what felt like days.

Jayne's good mood was fading fast, and I didn't

blame her for getting a little cranky. For almost an hour she'd been sitting on the floor, with her knees pulled up to her chest, to give me the greatest possible room to maneuver.

The size of department store dressing rooms is one of the great crimes of the universe. Right up there with the fact that concert halls and stadiums never have enough stalls in the girls' bathroom. If I were to design a dressing room, I'd most definitely include a spectator's chair in the layout. I mean, who goes shopping alone? Boring!

"I'm not talking about the *color*," I said, returning my attention to the mirror. "I'm referring to the fact that I look like I've been attacked by a spandex spray gun."

I had to admit that the dress showed off my figure. My waist looked tiny, and since the hem was practically up to my butt, my legs seemed longer. My hair (which I call dirt brown but others describe as chestnut) and deep brown eyes stood out against the bright red spandex. My skin even looked slightly tanned, which was a miracle considering the fact that I live in Seattle, Washington, a.k.a. the Rain Capital of the Western World. Still, I looked more like a girl auditioning for a VJ on MTV than someone who was dressed for a high-school dance.

Jayne studied the dress for a moment. "As a rule, spandex has no style," she announced. "Unlike silk, it leaves nothing to the imagination."

I agreed with Jayne, but I was so desperate to find the perfect outfit that I'd been hoping she'd convince me that this particular garment was the one for me.

2

"Why don't you just tell me I look like the Sleeze Babe of the Year and be done with it?" I asked.

Jayne shrugged. "You look like Tanya Wright—which is even worse than looking like the Sleeze Babe of the Year."

Now I *knew* Jayne was in a bad mood. She was well aware that the mere mention of Tanya's name was enough to take away my appetite for a week. But I decided to ignore her comment and keep my thoughts focused where they should be. On Dean Smith.

In my opinion, the fact that Dean had asked me out was nothing short of a miracle—particularly considering everything that had already happened between us.

Or, to be more accurate, what *hadn't* happened.

"Looks like it's back to the racks," I said as I reached down to pull the dress upward. "Maybe I'll get lucky and some girl will have just defaulted on a layaway."

"Maybe," Jayne responded. "But I doubt it."

I tugged the dress hard, trying to pull it up and over my head. Instead I found myself trapped in a spandex prison.

"Jayne, you've got to help me," I begged. "I think this dress is *alive*."

Jayne is not my best friend for nothing. Even when she's feeling less than perky, she comes to my defense. Probably because she's a Pisces. They're very loyal and sensitive. The Pisces motto is I Believe.

I'm a Scorpio. Our motto is I Desire. Ruled by our hearts, we're passionate and hot-blooded. At the moment this particular Scorpio was starting to feel that this dress was permanently attached to my body.

My entire future in bright red spandex flashed before my eyes: I would ride in the parade at the Strawberry Festival and the Tomato Festival. At Christmastime I'd put on little black boots and get a job at the mall as one of Santa's elves.

"I don't suppose you've got a can opener on you, do you?" I asked Jayne. *Or a pair of sharp scissors.*

She shook her head. "Hold still, Natalie. I'm going to try something."

Jayne gripped the bottom of the dress tightly. "On the count of three, I'm going to yank this thing over your head," she warned.

"Let's just hope this works," I said.

"One . . . two . . . three!"

I held my arms straight over my head, then bent down as Jayne tugged hard on the slippery material. Within seconds the dress was off my body. The material lay in a bright red heap in the corner of the dressing room.

"I think we killed it," Jayne said.

Finally free from the constraints of the dress, I took a deep, full breath. "It was a mercy killing, Jayne," I said. "Dr. Kevorkian would be proud of us."

She laughed. "Assisted suicide in the juniors' department of Kleinfeld's," she said in her best anchorwoman's voice. "See story at six."

"I never should have brought that thing in here in the first place." I picked up the dress, which now looked like a giant scrunchie, and put it back on its hanger. "I don't know what came over me."

"Fashion desperation," Jayne stated.

"Tell me about it," I said, pulling on my Levi's.

Jayne sighed. "I'm sorry I'm in such a bad mood. It's just—" She broke off, staring at herself in the mirror. "I wish we were picking out a dress for me too."

My shopping nightmare suddenly seemed totally unimportant. I knew from past experience that there was nothing more depressing than not having a date for a dance. And Jayne did *not* have a date.

As far as I'm concerned, Jayne is beautiful. She has soft blond hair and big blue eyes. But she's more comfortable with a book than she is with a guy. She has a bad habit of making herself look as drab as possible so that she'll blend into the crowd—which isn't the best way to get a date for anything, much less a Valentine's Day dance.

"Hey," I said, trying to sound upbeat. "At least *you* don't have to spend a lot of money on some fancy dress you'll only get to wear once."

"At the rate you're going, neither do you."

She was right. If I didn't find the perfect outfit soon, I was going to have to make do with what was already hanging in my closet.

I shook my head. "I don't know what's wrong with me. I never have any trouble shopping." I pulled on my own purple tank top. "I just don't understand why I can't find anything."

"Maybe you're nervous," Jayne suggested.

"Of course I'm nervous," I told her through the thick wool of the black turtleneck sweater I was struggling into. "I already screwed things up with Dean once. I can't afford to do it again."

"You didn't screw up," Jayne countered. "What

5

happened with Garth was totally unexpected. Nobody could blame you for that."

Dean had been a new student at the beginning of the school year. From the moment I'd set eyes on him in first-period English, things between us had clicked.

I'd floated through September in a pleasant haze of anticipation, daydreaming about the way this one lock of dark hair always fell across Dean's perfectly shaped forehead. And there always seemed to be something hidden in his smoky gray eyes. I was sure Dean was going to ask me out. I just didn't know *when*. Then something happened that had made me forget Dean Smith even existed.

Tanya Wright had broken up with Garth Hunter.

Garth and Tanya were what Jayne called an A-list couple. Their relationship was always the talk of the junior class. Bigger than life. And although Garth and Tanya were constantly fighting, nobody ever expected them to actually break up.

And when they *did* break up, I certainly didn't expect the unthinkable to occur. But it did. Garth turned to me.

I'd had a crush on Garth Hunter for as long as I could remember. Probably since I'd first learned how to breathe. All it had taken was one word, one look from Garth, and Dean Smith had been history.

Dean could have had three heads and three sets of beautiful, big gray eyes. I never would have noticed. Garth was the only guy I could see.

Unfortunately what I didn't notice was that our whole relationship was little more than a joke. We went out on a few dates and had a really great time . . . or so I thought. As it turned out, Garth just used me to get back at Tanya. As soon as she came crawling back to him, Garth dumped me.

"Natalie," Jayne said quietly, her voice full of understanding. She could probably see the way my whole painful history with Dean and Garth was scrolling just inside my eyes.

"You made a mistake," Jayne continued. "Everybody makes them. Dean doesn't seem to hold it against you, so why should you let it get you down?"

"I'm a Scorpio," I said feebly.

"Oh, no," Jayne said. "You promised, not while we're shopping. No astrology."

Astrology is the one and only topic on which Jayne and I do not agree. I think it's the perfect explanation for just about everything. She thinks it's a lot of bull.

But it was astrology that finally helped me get over Garth. Studying the stars and alignment of the planets made me understand the importance of looking beneath a person's exterior to find out what they're like inside. Some people use pop psychology to help them dissect the personalities of the people in their lives. I preferred to focus on the traits of a person's astrological sign.

If I'd been into astrology before I was stupid enough to go out with Garth, I'd have known that our relationship was destined for disaster. Our signs are totally incompatible!

I'm a Scorpio (Oct. 23–Nov. 21).

He's a Gemini (May 21–June 20).

Geminis are charming, but they're totally unpredictable. In Garth's case unpredictable was synonymous with untrustworthy.

7

Usually I tried to talk Jayne out of her narrow-minded views of astrology. But tonight I simply didn't have the time. If I didn't find a dress soon, I was going to have to spend the rest of the evening with the dictionary, making up the name of some previously unheard of and very rare disease. Then I'd cough until my throat was hoarse, call Dean, and tell him I had to break our date.

But I didn't want to do that. I wanted to go out with Dean—more than I'd wanted to do anything in a long, long time.

"Natalie, about this not being able to find a dress thing," Jayne began. "What were you thinking of while you were shopping?"

The answer to her question was obvious. "Naturally I was thinking about Dean."

"Aha!" Jayne said. I could almost see the light-bulb going off above her head.

"And just what does 'aha!' mean?" I asked. Sometimes I had a hard time following Jayne's line of thinking. She tends to get a bit abstract.

"You've been concentrating on the wrong thing. You've been trying to figure out what *Dean* would like."

"Of course I've been trying to figure out what Dean would like. He's my date, Jayne."

"But we already know what Dean likes," Jayne insisted.

"We do?"

"Natalie," Jayne said, in the same tone of voice she uses when I've failed to understand what she considers a perfectly straightforward math problem (though in my opinion there's no such thing as a

8

straightforward math problem). "Dean likes *you*."

I thought about what she'd said for a moment. Maybe Jayne was right. Maybe the reason nothing had looked right on me was because I was trying too hard.

"You're saying if I just pick out what I like, then Dean will like it?"

Jayne nodded. "That's what I'm saying."

"But that's too simple."

"You know what they say about the shortest distance between two points, don't you?" Jayne asked, crossing her arms in front of her chest.

I bit my lip. "That there's always something in the way?"

"In your life, probably yes," Jayne answered with a laugh. "In the real world, no."

"Oh, all right," I said. "I get the picture. I'll try to think *less* and just search for a dress I like *more*." I paused. "Okay, let's go out and try again. I'm looking for something feminine and sexy."

"But not too blatant," Jayne added.

I nodded. "My dress should have a little bit of mystery." Actually the description was sounding pretty good.

I was ready . . . for anything.

Late Friday night I sat in bed, listening to the rain drip from the eaves outside my window. I was waiting impatiently for my digital clock to click over to 12:00 A.M.

At 12:00 A.M. it would be Valentine's Day. February 14. The day of my first date with Dean.

I hadn't intended to stay up this late. In fact, I

was kind of worried about the potential lack of sleep. I didn't want to go to the Sweethearts' Dance looking like a raccoon. But I couldn't seem to go to sleep, and finally I'd given up the struggle.

Besides, I figured if I was awake at midnight, I could allow myself to read my Valentine's Day horoscope.

I used to read my horoscope just for fun. But that was before I got into astrology. Now I pay serious attention to it. It's the first thing I do every day.

Reading my forecast is a very grounding experience. It helps me realize that everything in the universe is connected. The position of a star or planet all the way across the solar system had the ability to seriously impact my life.

There was a special reason for my wanting to read my Valentine's forecast, of course. I wanted to see if there was anything relating to my upcoming date with Dean.

I glanced at the digital clock sitting on my nightstand. I've always thought it's bad luck to read any day's forecast even a second early. The green numbers read 11:59. As I watched they changed positions. 12:00. At last. The waiting was over. I opened the drawer of my nightstand and pulled out my astrological forecast.

Scorpios are born between October 23 and November 21. But as every student of astrology knows, these dates aren't set in stone. Some years they change by as much as a day. It all depends on the position of the stars and planets in the sky.

A single minute has the ability to determine under which sign a person is born. And if a person is born on the cusp, chances are he or she will have some characteristics of both signs: the sign just ending and the sign just beginning. I didn't have to worry about any of that, though. I was born on November fifth, right in the middle of the sign of Scorpio.

Scorpios feel things more intensely than other people, with the possible exception of Leos. Scorpio is also a fixed sign. That means we're stubborn, focused, and persevering. Once we make up our minds, we don't back down.

Stop dwelling in the past and look toward tomorrow, my horoscope started. *Your reward could be new love. But old habits die hard, particularly where your heart is concerned. Taurus individual could play a healing role.*

I set the newspaper down, considering my forecast. Most of it sounded pretty good, especially that sentence about new love. And the fact that there might be a Taurus in the picture was a definite plus.

Taurus (April 20–May 20) is my astral opposite. My perfect astrological mate. Taurians are very practical and down-to-earth. In fact, Taurus is a fixed earth sign. That makes them the perfect balance for Scorpio—fixed earth grounding fixed water.

I made a mental note to make sure Dean was really a Taurus. But I wasn't too worried. All my instincts told me that he was. He hadn't given up on me all through that horrible Garth business. And then there was the fact that he'd asked me to the dance. . . .

"Natalie, wait up!" Dean had yelled a couple of weeks ago as I climbed the front steps of Emerald High School.

Because it's so green, Seattle is nicknamed the

Emerald City; hence the origin of the name of our school. Emerald students, however, claim the school got its name for another reason—the green slime that always seems to be slithering down the bathroom walls.

Dean's jacket was wet, and he had raindrops caught in his eyelashes. I wondered if he could hear the way my heart suddenly started to pound.

I'd been trying to think of a way to show Dean that I was over Garth, but I hadn't been able to come up with a solid plan. Dean had never actually asked me out, so it wasn't like I'd cheated on him or anything. It was more like I'd cheated on the *possibility* of him.

"Doesn't it ever stop raining?" Dean had complained as the door of Emerald High slammed shut behind us.

"Not in February," I told him. "Last year it rained twenty-six out of twenty-eight days."

"That's it," he'd said. "I'm moving back to Arizona. Down there we really appreciate a good *sand*storm."

I'd laughed and started down the hall to first-period English. "Hey, Natalie," Dean had called after me. "I was wondering—"

I'd stopped and turned around. Dean's face looked a little tense but very determined. "Do you have a date yet for the Sweethearts' Dance?"

And that had been it. No making me feel bad for what had or hadn't happened between us. No mention of Garth Hunter at all. In that second I'd known that Dean was a Taurus. And He hadn't become emotional and spiteful, but remained level-headed about everything in classic Taurus style. Right away I'd known my instincts about him hadn't been

12

wrong. We could really have a future together.

So what is all this business about dwelling in the past? I wondered as I glanced back down at my horoscope.

I thought about the forecast for a few minutes, watching the numbers on my clock slide toward 12:30. Finally I got out of bed. The hardwood floor was cold, but I didn't bother with my bedroom slippers. I was on a mission.

I tiptoed across my room and opened the bottom drawer of my dresser. Hidden under my patiently-waiting-for-summer T-shirts was an old stationery box with an embossed gold lid. I pulled out the box and got back into bed. Very gently I eased the lid open.

Inside was every single memento of my life with Garth.

Mostly I had clippings taken from the school newspaper. I'd saved everything about Garth that had ever been written. There was the article that showed him running for student council. (He'd lost, but he hadn't been at all embarrassed.) Another article was accompanied by a photo that showed him sitting on the bench after he'd been fouled out of a basketball game.

But the one I'd loved the most was a picture of the two of us together. It had been taken just last fall, at Homecoming.

Garth's arm was slung around my shoulders. He was smiling at the camera. I was smiling up at him. There was so much love in my face, a blind person could have seen it.

But with the exception of the expression on my face, everything about the photograph had been a fake.

The picture in the *Emerald Times* had been Garth's revenge on Tanya. Physical proof that he didn't care about the fact that she'd dumped him.

And when Tanya had seen the picture of Garth with his arm around another girl on the front page of the school newspaper, she'd done exactly what Garth wanted. She'd come crawling back to him.

Why do I still have these? I asked myself as I stared down at Garth's triumphant sneer. Even now, looking at that photograph made my heart squeeze in pain. Not pain over losing Garth—but pain that I'd been so stupid. From the start I should have been smart enough to see that Garth was a piece of scum.

My horoscope is right, I thought. I wasn't really moving forward. As long as I held on to these memories of Garth, I was still living in the past.

This time when I got out of bed, I slid my feet into my furry red bedroom slippers. I also put on my thick terry-cloth robe. Then I tiptoed downstairs, being careful not to wake my parents. I had less than no desire to explain to my mom why I was wandering through the house in the middle of the night with a box stuffed under my arm.

But I knew what I had to do. I headed for the kitchen and lifted up the lid of the garbage can. Then I emptied my entire box of Garth memorabilia into the trash.

The past was dead. It was time to bury it.

I got an old spatula from a kitchen drawer. Then I carefully pushed every single picture of Garth underneath a pile of wet coffee grounds.

Two

Dean

Gemini (May 21–June 20)
Fresh start! The opportunity you've been waiting
for is just around the corner. Now is your time to
right old wrongs. Don't let your enthusiasm lead you
astray, however. When in doubt, take your time.

"I LOOK LIKE an idiot," I said, looking at myself in the bathroom mirror. I was trying without success to insert my finger between my too tight shirt collar and my Adam's apple. What is it about formal wear? Magazine advertisers would have the general population believe that tuxedos are supposed to make a guy look romantic. But I think a tux stifles a guy's ability, not to mention will, to breathe.

"You do seem a bit discomfited," John Muirhead, my best friend, said from the doorway. John has a 4.0 grade point average. He likes to use the kind of vocabulary words that I usually encounter only on English quizzes.

"I think I'm being strangled to death," I moaned.

"You look like a booger head," my little brother, Randy, shouted helpfully from his bedroom.

"A booger *brain*," his twin, Roy, corrected him.

I could hear John making odd choking sounds from the other side of the doorway. I assumed it was because he was trying not to laugh. For some unknown reason, he finds my little brothers endlessly amusing. Probably because he doesn't have to live with them.

"You actually look like a *dummy*, Dean," John said. "You should be made of wood and sitting on the knee of some misguided ventriloquist."

"Dummy Dean!" Roy shouted.

I heard a burst of loud giggles. Great. Now I was going to spend at least the next six months as "Dummy Dean."

"Thanks a lot, John," I muttered.

"Don't mention it," John said.

I'd finally managed to get my finger inside my shirt collar. I gave it a gentle tug. The bow tie I'd just spent the last twenty minutes perfecting crumpled—but at least I could breathe.

There has to be a trick to this, I thought as I wrestled the tie back into submission. Something known to every guy in the entire universe but me. Right now I wished that I'd broken down and bought the clip-on bow tie I'd seen at the tuxedo rental place.

I groaned. "How come I thought I wanted to go to a formal?" I asked John. "Will you please remind me?"

"No red-blooded American guy *wants* to go to a formal," John asserted. "You were willing to make the sacrifice so you wouldn't lose out on your

16

best opportunity to ask out Natalie Taylor."

John was right, of course. Not that I intended to admit that he'd read my mind once again. Valentine's Day had seemed like the perfect chance to get close to Natalie.

I'd wanted to take her out for months, ever since the moment I'd seen her in first-period English. She'd been laughing at a joke somebody else had told just before I came into the room. Her big, brown eyes had been warm and open—even though I hadn't heard the joke, I'd felt like joining in her laughter.

Now that's a girl I'd like to know better, I'd thought.

Unfortunately for me, I hadn't got up the nerve to act on my initial attraction for quite a while. I don't like to do things in a hurry. I never have. I prefer to act when I feel I have firm ground beneath my feet. If nothing else, I know what it's going to feel like when I fall.

My mother says the fact that I don't rush into things is a good quality. "Slow and steady wins the race, Dean." My mother is full of hokey clichés. She has one for almost every occasion.

But in the case of Natalie Taylor, not only had I lost the race, I didn't even make it to the playing field. Just about the time I'd gotten up my courage to ask Natalie for a date, there had been a small diversion. A diversion named Garth Hunter.

Then I'd had to wait three months for Natalie even to remember I existed again.

I'd waited another month to ask her out—just to be sure there weren't any aftershocks following her brief relationship with Garth. Finally I'd decided I couldn't afford to wait past Valentine's Day.

But now Valentine's Day was here, and I was staring at myself in the bathroom mirror, feeling completely nervous.

"Come on, Dean," John called. "You have to come out of there sometime."

I stepped out into the hall. "Hey, you don't look too bad," John commented. He put his head on one side, like he was considering a scientific experiment. "Nice cummerbund."

I brushed past him on my way back to my bedroom. "Gee, thanks." I grabbed my wallet off my dresser and tucked it into my pants pocket.

"Someday you'll be wearing all this gear. Then it will be my turn to torture you with snide comments."

John flopped down across my bed. "Me in a tuxedo?" he scoffed. "No way!"

I turned around to face him. "Never say never. All you have to do is meet the right girl."

John studied the pattern on my bedspread. "I don't think there is a right girl out there for me."

Way to go, Dean, I scolded myself. *You had to go remind John that he's Dateless in Seattle.*

Unfortunately for John, he sort of looks like he's got a 4.0 GPA. I don't mean that he's a total geek. But he does have this major hair problem. The top of his head always looks like he's just been struck by lightning.

"Dean, it's almost seven," my mother's voice drifted down the hall. Her arrival put a stop to John's and my conversation. "You don't want to be late, honey." She poked her head into my room. "And don't forget this." She held out a small box.

During the day my mom is a high-powered ad

executive. But as soon as she gets home, she trades in her business suits for jeans and T-shirts. In honor of Valentine's Day, tonight she was wearing red sweatpants and a purple-and-gold University of Washington Huskies sweatshirt. She held a plastic florist's box, in which rested Natalie's corsage. My mom had insisted that we keep the corsage in the fridge, which was apparently the best way to keep it fresh. But all day long she'd been terrified that I'd go off without the flowers. As if.

My mother stopped short when she caught sight of me in the expensive, not to mention uncomfortable, rented tuxedo. She got this sort of misty, faraway look in her eyes. It was definitely a Kodak moment.

Then my little brother Randy stuck his head through the door of his room.

"Dean looks like a dummy," he announced.

"I think he looks wonderful," my mother answered.

"You're a mother. You have to say that," Randy said. He wrapped himself around my mother's legs and tugged on her sweatshirt. "Can we watch the movie we rented as soon as Dean's gone?"

"You rented a movie?" I asked. "That's it. I'm staying home."

"You can't," Randy responded, sticking out his tongue at me. "We only have enough ice cream to share with John."

Now that the moment of departure had arrived, I'd gone from feeling nervous to terrified.

I'd wanted to go out with Natalie for what seemed like forever, but what if something went wrong? Sometimes anticipating an event is better than the event itself. Not that I *seriously* thought that was going to be a problem. Not with Natalie Taylor.

"So," I said. "I guess I'd better get going." But my feet didn't move.

John pointed. "There's the door." His face held the smug smile of one who didn't have to spend the next five hours making first-date small talk.

I grabbed my keys off the dresser. "As of this moment, I'm making it my number-one priority to find you a date for the prom," I told John.

"Have a really good time, honey," my mother called as I started down the hall. "I'll try not to get all sentimental and wait up for you to come home."

Roy stuck his head out the door of his bedroom. "Good night, booger brain," he called.

I wondered if other guys were fortunate enough to have such loving families or if I was the only one.

"Dean," my mother called out just before I escaped from the house. "Aren't you forgetting something?"

I stopped and ran through my mental checklist. Tuxedo. Car keys. Cash. Corsage . . .

Oops. I'd forgotten to take the box with Natalie's corsage in it. As I headed back up the stairs toward my bedroom I heard John's laughter—along with the laughter of every member of my family.

"I can't believe this," I said several hours later. Natalie and I were standing near the entrance to the Emerald High gym, under a wooden trellis decorated with red silk roses. Nearby a small tape recorder was playing bird sounds. I think the chirping was supposed to help set the mood, but I kept having an almost irrepressible urge to giggle. Particularly with the bass of Ginger Ross, the band playing at the dance, thumping away in the background.

"I can't believe I let you talk me into getting my picture taken," I continued to Natalie.

"I can't believe you're being such a baby about it," she replied. I looked down at her, trying to think of a snappy comeback. At that moment the flashbulb went off.

"Ooh, perfect," the photographer exclaimed.

"There, now," Natalie said, tucking her arm through mine. "That wasn't so bad, was it?"

"Not unless you're worried about those giant white spots before my eyes."

Natalie laughed. The sound was light and easy. So far, the evening had been an unqualified success. Natalie and I had been joking and talking as if we'd known each other for years.

I'd known things were going to go well from the moment I'd picked her up. Natalie looked incredible. She was wearing an amazing black dress, which was made out of a not-quite-see-through material.

The dress made me want to take a second look at Natalie. And then a third look. And a fourth. In fact, I'd been so blown away by how beautiful Natalie looked, I'd almost forgotten to give her the corsage.

I'd worried a little about the flowers. A corsage of red rosebuds and white baby's breath wasn't very original. But the arrangement had turned out to be perfect. The corsage matched a spray of red rosebuds that were tucked into her upswept hair.

"All right now," the photographer called over

the fake chirping of the birds. "We're ready for our second shot."

"Smile for the birdie," I whispered.

"Smile for the birdie," the photographer sang out. As if on cue, the birds on the tape began to warble frantically. This time Natalie and I were both laughing as the flash went off.

"I wish Jayne had been here to see that," Natalie commented a few minutes later. We were sitting at a small bistro table lit by a red heart-shaped candle. The band was taking a break, so Natalie and I were hanging out and drinking punch.

"Jayne," I said. "You mean Jayne Engerman?"

Natalie nodded.

"Isn't she here tonight?"

Natalie took a sip of punch and shook her head. "I wish. I swear sometimes I think every guy at Emerald must have attention deficit disorder or something. Not one of them has ever noticed how really great she is."

"Hey, don't think you can blame everything on guys," I protested, feeling the need to come to the defense of my gender. Not that Natalie wasn't right about a lot of guys, of course. But I could hardly take a comment like that one lying down. I'd be kicked out of the testosterone union.

"I know a guy who's really awesome," I continued. "And not one girl has ever noticed *him*."

"Oh yeah? Who?" Natalie asked, her eyes sparkling.

"John Muirhead."

"Smartest guy in the entire universe John Muirhead?"

"That's the one. It just so happens he'd love to

go out on dates. But not one girl I know of will even look at him."

"I'll bet Jayne would," Natalie challenged. "She's just as smart as he is. They probably have lots in common. I'll bet all we'd have to do would be to get them together and they'd fall head over heels in love."

"That's ridiculous," I said. "You can't plan love at first sight." Of course, John and Jayne already knew of each other's existence—I was sure that they had several advanced-placement classes together.

Natalie looked at me over the rim of her punch glass, her eyes laughing. "Chicken."

There is one major quirk in my slow and steady personality. I absolutely cannot resist a dare.

"All right, let's do it," I said. After all, what did I have to lose? The worst thing that could happen was that the four of us would get together and Jayne and John would totally ignore each other.

"How do you want to work this?" I asked.

Natalie considered the question for a moment. I could hear the band start to play in the background. Natalie tapped her foot in time to the bass.

"Jayne and I are going out for coffee at about one o'clock tomorrow afternoon," she finally answered. "If you guys just happened to show up at the espresso bar—would that look too planned?"

"I don't think so," I said, mulling it over. "Particularly if you guys went to Bob's Buzz Stop."

"The coffee at Café Luna is better," Natalie informed me. "But I think I could put up with Bob's Buzz Stop in the interest of true love."

"Okay, so we're on. One o'clock tomorrow at Bob's Buzz Stop."

Natalie nodded. "Great. If they click, you have to take me to the Luna Sunday afternoon for the rest of the month."

"If they don't, you have to buy," I said. This was good. Natalie was already making plans to see me again.

"Shake on it," Natalie said, extending her arm across the table. I took her hand in mine. Her fingers were cool from holding the cold glass of punch.

"Well," said a voice above our heads. "You two certainly look like you're having a good time."

Natalie's head jerked up. Her fingers tightened around mine. "Oh, hi, Tanya," she said without much enthusiasm.

Tanya Wright looks like a fashion model. She's tall and skinny and has bleached blond hair. She looked as if she'd been painted in her tight red dress. As Natalie took in the details of Tanya's appearance a strange expression came over her face.

I wasn't sure what Tanya wanted. Probably just to make Natalie feel as uncomfortable as possible. Tanya's the vindictive type. She'll hold a grudge forever. And I figured she'd never forgive Natalie for going out with Garth.

I'd hoped to be able to avoid Garth Hunter. I just didn't see any point in putting myself into a situation where Natalie could make a direct comparison between the two of us.

Garth was the kind of guy girls fill up entire diaries swooning over. Compared to him, I was Mr. Slow-and-Steady-Wins-the-Race Dean.

An arm in a black jacket snaked around Tanya's waist. "Ooh, Garth, you scared me," she squealed. I wondered how she could inhale any air, her dress was so tight.

Natalie stood up quickly, her hand still holding mine tightly. "How about another dance, Dean?" Her cheeks were flushed, but I couldn't tell if she was angry or upset.

"Sounds great to me." I stood up and followed her toward the dance floor.

"You two have a great time out there," Garth called after us. "Don't do anything I wouldn't do, Dean."

I wouldn't take a girl like Natalie out just to dump her, I thought. *If that's what you mean.*

Natalie kept walking until we were in the middle of the dance floor. Then she stopped so suddenly, I almost ran right into her. Before I knew what was happening, she turned and wrapped her arms around me.

"Oh, Dean." She sighed. Was her voice sad? Frustrated? I couldn't tell.

I put my arms around her and swayed in time to the music. As the band launched into the next slow number I tried not to worry too much about what Natalie had meant when she'd murmured, "Oh, Dean."

Slow dancing with Natalie was like nothing I'd ever experienced. She fit into my arms as if we'd been made to dance together. She didn't hang on like she was drowning, the way some girls did. And she didn't crowd me so that our knees knocked together.

She just fit. My arms made a perfect circle around her waist. Hers made a perfect circle around my neck. Two seconds after the dance started, I forgot all about Garth Hunter. He couldn't come between us. Not when Natalie felt this good in my arms.

What would it feel like to kiss her? My heart pounded as I stared at Natalie's smooth, soft lips. More than anything I wanted to kiss Natalie senseless—until I was the only guy she even remembered existed on the planet.

Slowly I lowered my head and brushed my lips down the side of Natalie's neck. A shiver ran up my spine. Natalie sighed softly and leaned back her head. I looked down into her eyes.

Natalie's eyes were warm, like hot bittersweet chocolate. She was smiling when her lips met mine.

Kissing Natalie was like diving into deep water. There was a sudden jolt as our lips met, followed by a long, slow glide. I could taste her lipstick and the cherry punch. The combination was addictive.

I almost didn't notice when the song was over. I could have stood on the dance floor forever, holding Natalie in my arms. As our lips parted I wasn't sure whether or not Natalie been kissed senseless. But I knew I had.

"So does this mean you'll be my girlfriend?" I whispered in her ear.

"Just try to stop me."

"Doesn't the sky look amazing tonight?" Natalie asked an hour later. "There are stars everywhere."

The Sweethearts' Dance was over, and I was driving Natalie home. My arm was stretched across the back of the front seat of my mom's Toyota Camry. Natalie was sitting *right* next to me with her head against my shoulder. I could see her face every time we passed beneath a streetlight.

It was late, and Natalie's tree-lined street was quiet. As I pulled into her driveway I noticed that Natalie's parents had left the porch light on. Another light glowed in a corner of the living room. I wondered if Mrs. Taylor was waiting up—like I was sure my mom was.

The thought of our good-night kiss had my heart hammering against the inside of my chest. I wondered if it was too soon to ask Natalie if I could see her again. Like maybe in about twenty seconds.

"We'd better not sit out here too long," Natalie commented as I switched off the ignition. "My mom probably has the video camera aimed at the car."

"That's nothing," I confided. "My mom bought night vision goggles this afternoon."

Natalie turned to face me. With warm fingers she brushed the bangs off my forehead. I could tell she was thinking of a way to beat the night vision goggles. "My dad has access to the Hubble Telescope," she said.

I made a split second decision. "You win," I said. "I don't really have a dad."

Natalie's hand stopped moving on my forehead. I reached up and covered her fingers with mine.

"I'm really sorry, Dean," she said. "I mean—oh, gosh, now I feel stupid."

"Don't apologize," I said. "There's no way you could have known. He walked out on us when I was little."

Natalie's dark brown eyes were fixed on my face. "That's rough. Life really sucks sometimes, doesn't it?"

I nodded. "Big time."

The light on the front porch began to flicker. Natalie put her head down on my shoulder and groaned. "I can't believe it. I am going to have to kill my parents."

"I have the perfect weapon. One of my little brothers left his stinky tennis shoes in the trunk of the car."

As soon as we got out of the Camry the porch light stopped blinking. I walked Natalie to the front porch but stopped short of the door. We were near the light, but not quite in it. Hopefully Mr. and Mrs. Taylor couldn't see us *too* clearly.

"So I'll see you tomorrow, huh?" I said. I wrapped my arms around her waist and pulled her close. "One P.M., Bob's Buzz Stop."

Natalie nodded. "You'd better come prepared to lose." Then her gaze moved above my head. "Oh, Dean, look!" she cried, shifting in my arms suddenly. "Look up! There's a shooting star."

I followed her line of vision just in time to see a streak of light go arcing across the sky.

"Shooting stars are supposed to bring good luck," Natalie whispered.

"They're nothing but space dust," I whispered back.

Natalie laughed. "You're terrible," she said. "I bet there's not a romantic bone in your whole body."

"Oh, yes, there is," I said.

"Prove it," she whispered, moving her face a little closer.

I may not be a genius, but I know opportunity when I see it. I lowered my head and met Natalie's lips with my own.

"Happy Valentine's Day." I murmured.

Three

NATALIE

Scorpio (Oct. 23–Nov. 21)
Romantic cycle riding high. Emphasis on your love
life and that of someone close to you. Don't let your
passionate Scorpio nature lead you on a wild-goose
chase. Use your energies to focus on your goal.

"HOW COME WE'RE going here?" Jayne asked
as I pushed open the door of Bob's Buzz
Stop. "You don't even like this place."

"Maybe I want to give it another chance," I said,
heading toward the order counter. "After all, it's a
woman's prerogative to change her mind."

I eyed the pastries in the large glass case, then
decided to just get coffee. I didn't want Dean to
come in and discover me with powdered sugar all
over my mouth.

"As a young feminist I resent that remark," Jayne
stated. She ordered her usual grande mocha, no whip.
"It perpetuates the myth that women have no minds."

"Double tall nonfat vanilla latte," I said to the woman behind the counter. "Relax, Jayne. I was just joking."

I gazed around Bob's Buzz Stop, taking in the decor. The place really wasn't all that bad. I would never like it as much as Café Luna, but it did have a certain scruffy charm.

Techno–New Age was the best way to describe Bob's Buzz Stop. Posters for alternative-rock band concerts and New Age businesses lined the walls. There was even a row of computer stations set up in one corner. In front of monitors computer geeks guzzling coffee surfed the Net.

"Oh, fine, abuse me," Jayne said as we paid for our drinks and headed to a table by the window. "This is what I came out in the rain for?"

The clouds had rolled in Sunday morning, and by the time I'd woken up, it had absolutely begun to pour. It was almost as if the gods of rain were angry that they'd lost a whole twenty-four hours of bad weather on Valentine's Day—now they were determined to make up for lost time.

Inside, the windows of Bob's Buzz Stop were fogged up from a combination of steam rising from the patrons as well as from the espresso machine.

"No," I said as we settled into our seats. "You came out because you're my best friend, and you're dying to hear about my date with Dean."

And because you're going to help me win my bet, I added silently. When I'd thought about the challenge I'd issued Dean last night, I'd realized it might be considered kind of tacky to place a bet on my very best friend.

Luckily I'd managed to console myself with the knowledge that the bet was for Jayne's own good. And winning was really only a secondary consideration. The most important aspect of my mission was to help Jayne fall in love.

"So how was it?" Jayne asked, taking a sip of her mocha.

"Fabulous, incredible, wonderful," I answered. "Engerman, you've got whipped cream on your nose."

Jayne wiped her face off with a napkin. "Fabulous, incredible, wonderful. Is that all?"

"Tanya wore that red dress," I said. My jaw had practically dropped to the floor when I'd realized that Tanya was wearing the same dress I'd tried on at Kleinfeld's.

Jayne came close to choking on her mocha. "Natalie Taylor, you lie."

"I do not," I said. "Wait until Monday morning—she probably won't have managed to peel it off her body yet." I paused for a millisecond. "Jayne, just before Dean kissed me good night we saw a shooting star."

Fortunately for me Jayne is used to my lightning-swift changes in conversation topics. They're one of the hallmarks of the sign of Scorpio.

"I hope she's stuck in that dress for the rest of her life," Jayne answered. "And for your information, shooting stars are nothing more than astral dust rhinos. Did Dean ask if he could see you again?"

A blast of cold air hit the table as the door of Bob's Buzz Stop opened.

"Hey, Natalie. Hey, Jayne," a casual voice called. "I didn't know you guys hung out here."

Dean was a better actor than I'd anticipated. Jayne was never going to suspect the meeting was a setup. And if she did, she'd think I'd made us come here in the hopes of running into Dean—not into Dean's best friend.

"You guys know John Muirhead, don't you?" Dean continued, walking over to our table.

"Sure," I answered, smiling. "Hi, John."

John's hair looked like a cyclone had hit it. But I noticed he had really nice brown eyes.

"Same to you," John answered. "I mean, hi." His gaze slid from me to Jayne. Jayne held John's eyes for a moment, then swallowed and looked back down at her cup. Two spots of hot red color burned along her cheekbones. I raised an eyebrow. Jayne *never* blushed—not even when she was embarrassed.

Victory, I thought. *Dean Smith, prepare to lose this bet.*

"Why don't you guys go get something to drink," I suggested. "Then come sit with us."

"Sounds great," Dean responded, his gray eyes smiling. "Come on, John." He clapped a hand on John's back and steered him over to the espresso counter.

"Natalie," Jayne hissed as soon as the guys were out of earshot. "What are you doing?"

"I'm being nice," I said. "What's wrong with that? Don't tell me you're going to deprive me of a chance to sit with Dean."

Jayne's eyes flickered toward the counter. I sipped my latte, watching her trying *not* to watch John. "You don't really mind them coming to sit with us, do you?" I asked after a minute. "I mean, John Muirhead does have a reputation of being kind of a nerd. . . ."

Jayne's eyes darted back to me, her whole face suffused with bright red color. "John Muirhead is not a nerd. Just because a guy is smart—" She broke off the sentence with a sigh. "Honestly, Natalie, I can't believe you'd be so shallow."

I put up my hands in a gesture of surrender. She'd reacted just the way I'd hoped she would. In fact, all this heavy blushing action had me thinking that perhaps Jayne had had a crush on John Muirhead all along.

"Okay," I said. "I take it all back. I'm sorry."

"They're coming back," Jayne announced. "We'd better shut up."

Dean and John snagged some empty chairs from a nearby table and sat down. I noticed that the guys had ordered the same drinks Jayne and I had. Dean had a latte like I did. John and Jayne both had mochas.

Dean pulled his chair next to mine so that our legs were touching. The light touch of his jean-clad leg against mine made the room all of a sudden feel very warm. For a moment we were all silent. All four of us seemed to be wondering who would speak up first.

"So, John," I finally said. "What's your astrological sign?"

If looks could kill, Jayne would have turned me into a corpse from across the table. John merely looked confused.

"Astrological sign?" he said.

"Sure. You know, the Age of Aquarius, that sort of stuff."

He nodded. "I'm a Pisces."

"Oh, really?" Hmmm . . . this piece of information was very interesting. I'd hoped John would say he was a Virgo, the perfect counterpart to Jayne's sign. But Jayne was a Pisces too.

"What's your birthday?" I asked.

"The third of March."

"March 3," Jayne echoed. "But that's the same as mine."

John turned his head in Jayne's direction. He looked right at her for the first time since he'd sat down. "It is? Really? That's incredible. Happy birthday."

"You too," Jayne said. "I mean, happy birthday."

They continued to stare at each other. I took a sip of latte and thought over what I'd learned.

Usually same-sign couples aren't a great combination. There's just not enough spark between them. They're too much alike. But the fact that Jayne and John were the same sign seemed to form the basis of their attraction. If nothing else, the fact that they had the same birthday gave them something to talk about.

"So," I said happily. "It looks like you two are soul mates."

Jayne scowled at me. "Don't pay any attention to Natalie," she told John. "She's got this astrology hang-up."

"Actually," John said, "I think the study of astrology is very interesting. Many ancient cultures were heavily influenced by the stars. The builders of Stonehenge, for example—"

"I thought Stonehenge was built to help plan the yearly planting cycle," Jayne interrupted.

"Well, yes," John admitted. "But that's not all. In fact, some scholars believe . . ."

Under the table Dean squeezed my hand. He

leaned forward so that Jayne and John couldn't overhear what he was going to say next.

"I guess you win the bet," he said. "Looks like I owe you some lattes."

I liked it that Dean didn't have the usual guy ego thing about always having to be the winner. "Actually I think it's a draw," I whispered back. "I'm getting the feeling that Jayne's been interested in John for a long time and I just never noticed."

With his thumb Dean began drawing small circles on the back of my hand. The feathery touch made my whole arm tingle. "How could you not notice a thing like that?" he asked.

"Maybe because I was busy noticing something else," I answered, smiling up into his incredible gray eyes.

Dean grinned. "I don't suppose you'd care to explain that remark."

"Well," I said, dropping my eyes demurely. "I have been worrying about this really big math test."

Dean laughed. I was about to tell him what had *really* been distracting me when a second burst of cold air swept across the table. I frowned. Garth and Tanya had just come through the door.

I must be cursed, I thought. All I wanted was to forget about Garth Hunter. The sight of him made my skin crawl. But it seemed as if I ran into him every time I turned around. If I hadn't known he was too egotistical to think of anyone but himself, I would have thought he was checking out my new potential boyfriend.

Dean's body stiffened as his gaze fell on Garth. I could feel the tension travel down his arm to where his hand was clutching mine. Garth and Tanya ignored us. They made their way up to the order counter. Jayne and John didn't seem to notice that both Dean and I were staring across the room. They were still discussing the purpose of Stonehenge.

"I can't stay long," Dean said. "I promised my mom I'd help out with my little brothers. I just came along to help out the course of true love," he added in a whisper.

I nodded. "That's okay. I understand."

I hoped Dean wasn't too bothered by Garth. Part of me wanted to come right out and tell Dean that he didn't have to worry about Garth—I was totally over him. But I was afraid that even mentioning Garth would make him seem too important to me.

All new relationships have tense moments, I told myself. After all, I wouldn't have been very happy if Dean had an old girlfriend—whom we kept running into all the time.

"So," I said to Dean. "I guess I'll see you in English tomorrow."

Dean smiled. "Wouldn't miss it," he said. "Mr. Dixon's lectures are *so* stimulating."

"If you happen to have the IQ of a frog," I countered.

Dean stood up. John tore his gaze away from Jayne and raised his eyebrows. "You're going?" John asked. He sounded disappointed.

Dean nodded. "I've got to get home. You can stay, though."

"Oh, no," John said. He stood up quickly. "Me too. I mean, I've got to go home."

I began to see why John had trouble getting dates. He seemed to crack a bit under pressure.

Obviously the thought of being left alone with two girls terrified him.

But I liked John. On a scale of one to ten I gave the afternoon a nine. Jayne had seemed genuinely absorbed in her somewhat esoteric conversation with John. And Dean and I showed no signs of cooling down.

"Later," Dean called over his shoulder as he walked toward the door of Bob's Buzz Stop.

"Later," John echoed.

"Bye!" Jayne and I called in unison.

And then they were gone. Jayne was quiet for a few moments. I was acutely aware of the empty spot beside me, where Dean had been sitting minutes before. I listened to the steamer make hissing noises from behind the bar.

"You like him, don't you?" I asked finally. There was no reason not to take the direct approach.

"Like who?" Jayne asked.

"You know who," I said. "You like John."

Jayne flipped her blond hair over one shoulder. "So what if I do?" she asked dryly.

"*So* I think it's great," I answered. "You're my best friend. John is Dean's best friend. Double dates, here we come."

Jayne was silent. She folded and refolded her paper napkin. "Do you really think he might ask me out?" she asked after a few seconds. "I mean, John Muirhead is, like, the smartest guy in the whole school."

"Perfect." I grinned. "Then he should be just about smart enough to deserve you."

Jayne smiled. "I knew there was a reason why you're my best friend. Now, I have just one more question."

"What's that?" I asked. I was expecting Jayne to inquire about the intricacies of French kissing.

"What's Dean's sign?"

"Romeo and Juliet are without a doubt the most famous lovers in all of literature," our English teacher, Mr. Dixon, informed the class Monday morning. Duh.

Mr. Dixon's voice was as condescending as ever. He sounded as if he thought none of his world literature students had heard of Romeo and Juliet. Or of William Shakespeare, for that matter.

But a person would have to be raised on the moon not to know who Romeo and Juliet were. They were the original teenage couple—and the perfect illustration of the fact that parents should butt out of their kids' love lives.

"Many scholars feel Romeo and Juliet are doomed and tragic figures," Mr. Dixon continued. "Personally, I think Shakespeare has given us a couple of typical teenagers on hormone overload."

He waited for somebody to laugh, but no one did. Dufus Dixon, as everybody calls him, has been teaching English at Emerald High forever. One rumor has it that the school was actually built around him. I suppose he knows his stuff, but nobody I know has ever been able to figure out why Mr. Dixon became a high-school teacher. He thinks teenagers are natural-born scum.

And in my opinion, Mr. Dixon was all wrong about Romeo and Juliet. Hormones weren't Romeo and Juliet's problem. The problem was in their stars. Shakespeare even calls them star-crossed lovers in the play. What more does anybody need to know?

I had the stars on my mind a lot this morning—even more than usual. After Jayne asked me about Dean's zodiac sign the day before, I realized that I still didn't know for sure under which stars Dean had been born. This was crucial information.

"Let's get going," Mr. Dixon instructed. "Open your books to page twenty-four."

I flipped open my copy of *Romeo and Juliet,* considering my options. I wanted to clear up the matter of Dean's sign as soon as possible. Preferably before the end of this class period.

It wasn't that I was really worried about it, exactly. I was sure Dean was a Taurus. But I wanted to confirm what I already knew. Then I could concentrate on other pressing matters. Like getting Dean to notice how great I looked in my new Levi's.

"Now, here's an example of what I was talking about," Mr. Dixon said. "Right here, in act I, scene 5. Romeo literally falls in love with Juliet at first sight."

What's wrong with that? I wondered as I eased my elbow onto Dean's desk. Out of the corner of my eye I caught his smile.

Dean looked awesome this morning. He was wearing a pair of faded jeans, and his charcoal gray sweater was the same color as his eyes. One stray lock of hair fell across his forehead. I had to stop myself from reaching up to brush it back.

I sneaked a glance at Mr. Dixon. He was standing at the front of the classroom, waving his arms. I leaned a little farther onto Dean's desk. There was no time like the present.

"Dean," I whispered. "What's your sign?"

39

Dean's eyes darted to Mr. Dixon. The Dufus hates it when anybody talks during class. Particularly if they talk while *he's* talking.

"What?" he whispered back.

I pitched my voice a little louder. "What's your sign?"

"Ah, Ms. Taylor, Mr. Smith," Mr. Dixon called from the front of the classroom. "I'm so pleased to discover you're both in good voice today."

I could feel my heart sink right down to my new leather work boots. Some diabolical punishment always descended upon students who broke Mr. Dixon's gag order. Scorpios aren't known for their patience, but I wished I had managed to wait until the end of class to speak to Dean.

"The best way to relish the power of Shakespeare's language is to hear the words spoken aloud," Mr. Dixon informed us. He seemed to be relishing the fact that he was about to humiliate Dean and me in front of the entire class.

Please, I thought. *Somebody tell me this isn't happening.*

Mr. Dixon was going to make us read out loud.

Reading out loud is right up there with scrubbing the toilet. Particularly when the material being read was Shakespeare. His plays never make any sense—at least, not the first time through. The words are so archaic that they seem almost in another language.

"Begin with line forty-nine, Mr. Smith."

Out of the corner of my eye I could see the edges of Dean's copy of *Romeo and Juliet* quiver. I couldn't tell if he was shaking from nerves or laughter. I told myself that I should look at Dean's face to read his mood, but I was too embarrassed. Dean was in trouble—because of me.

"We're waiting, Mr. Smith," Mr. Dixon continued. Dean cleared his throat. After a brief pause he began to read.

Not bad, I thought, after Dean stopped to take a breath. The way Dean read the lines, Shakespeare actually made sense.

I listened with rapt attention as Dean continued to read. After a few moments I allowed myself to imagine that he was Romeo and I was Juliet.

I could still remember the first time Dean and I had seen each other. We had met right here in Mr. Dixon's English class. From the first moment I had known that Dean was something special. There had been chemistry between us. We had clicked.

We really are like Romeo and Juliet, I told myself. One significant glance was all that Romeo and Juliet had needed to fall in love. But unlike Shakespeare's lovers, Dean and I weren't going to end up dying in each other's arms at the end of the story. We were going to have a happy ending. Together forever. Happily ever after.

"Mmm," Dean said. "You taste as delicious as I remember."

Dean and I were leaning against the big oak tree in my front yard. I had been a little worried that Dean would be mad about me getting us in trouble this morning, but so far he seemed anything but angry.

I laughed. "Great line. Do you use that on all the girls you kiss?"

"Ouch!" Dean said with a smile. "Do you have

41

any idea how deflating to my ego this is? You've just rejected my best line!"

"I am not a fish," I informed him. "I don't need a line."

Dean's smile widened. "I'll try to keep that in mind," he said in low voice. His lips brushed softly against mine. A shiver traveled up my spine, and I responded to the pressure of his mouth. If I were a computer, my circuit boards would have been in complete meltdown.

After several long moments Dean pulled away. "So, Natalie," he said. "You owe me an explanation. What was all that about in English this morning?"

Thank goodness, I thought. *He brought up the subject of astrology on his own—sort of. We must be on the same astral wavelength.*

"I just wanted to know what sign you are," I explained. "Sorry about the incredibly bad timing. I didn't mean to get you into trouble."

"Dixon is a total jerk," Dean stated. Then he leaned a little closer so he could look into my eyes. "You're really into this astrology stuff, aren't you?"

"I find it pretty interesting," I acknowledged.

"As interesting as the purpose behind the building of Stonehenge?"

"Dean," I said. "You're stalling."

"Okay, okay. If it's so important to you. I'm a Gemini."

I couldn't believe it.

Dean Smith, the love of my life, was a . . . Gemini. Completely the wrong astrological sign.

For the last few hours the word *Gemini* had echoed through my brain.

Dinner had been a blur of lasagna, salad, and thinking about Dean. My mom had to tell me three times that I'd spilled my water glass. I'd been so absorbed in my own thoughts that I had failed to notice my jeans were soaking up ice-cold water.

Thankfully dinner was over. I was sitting on my bed, trying to find a way out of the mess my life had suddenly become. But my mind seemed to be spinning in circles. I felt like a laboratory rat trapped in a maze. No matter which way I turned, I came up against a dead end.

Dean was the same sign as Garth Hunter. A Gemini.

I rolled over and groaned. My gaze traveled from one side of my room to the other. The place looked like a scene from *Twister*. Books and papers were scattered across my mint green wall-to-wall carpet.

In the last half hour I had reread every scrap of information I could find about the Scorpio–Gemini relationship.

"The Scorpio–Gemini relationship can be full of excitement." This was according to my favorite book, *Exploring Astrological Love Signs*.

Trying to hold on to mercurial Gemini poses just the kind of challenge hot-blooded Scorpios love. Gemini's charm is a perfect compliment for your passions. He can laugh away your darkest moods.

The charm is bound to wear off,

however, when you realize that a lasting relationship is unattainable. Your Gemini lover can never be anything more than a fickle flirt.

Best to get out now, before heartbreak occurs. If you want a stable relationship, look elsewhere in the zodiac.

Elsewhere, I thought. *Like Taurus, for example.* I had been so sure Dean was a loyal, trustworthy Taurus. How had I made such a terrible mistake? All my instincts had told me Dean was someone I could trust. He had seemed so different from Garth. And Dean *was* different—at least superficially.

But I had learned the hard way—by being tortured by Garth—that I couldn't judge a guy by how he seemed on the surface. Not if I expected my heart to survive. Dean and Garth were the same where it counted. Deep down inside.

And sooner or later Dean would dump me. He wouldn't be able to help himself. The fact that Dean was going to smash my heart into bits was dictated by the stars. In the end he would be another Garth Hunter. Astrological destiny was unavoidable, like taxes and bad school lunches. Dean hadn't broken my heart yet, but he was going to. It was just a matter of time.

I rolled off my bed and headed across the hallway to the bathroom. I splashed my face with cold water, rinsing my tear-stained face. As I patted my face dry with a fluffy terry-cloth towel I finally faced the truth.

There was only one way out of my present situation. I had been looking for an escape clause all night—but there wasn't one.

I refused to deliberately court a romantic catastrophe. I couldn't afford to have my heart broken a second time.

I had to stop myself from falling more deeply in love with Dean Smith. I had to break up with Dean—before he broke up with me.

Four

DEAN

Gemini (April 20–May 20)
Surprise events shake what previously seemed
like a sturdy foundation. Don't panic. Now is the
time to discover who you really are. One who
doesn't have your best interests at heart may
try to distract you. Avoid anger. Stay calm.

I DECIDED TO cruise by Café Luna before school
on Tuesday morning. It's not a place where I
usually hang out—there's too much of the wearing-
basic-black-and-looking-very-arty crowd.

But I knew Natalie liked Café Luna, so I was
willing to subject myself to a bunch of pretentious
people discussing vegetarianism and Kafka.
Hopefully I would run into Natalie.

"Natalie." I repeated the word to myself for the
tenth time that morning. I shook my head and
laughed. I had to stop myself from saying her name.
But I seemed physically incapable of thinking about

anything besides Natalie. This morning Roy had buried a cherry Gummi Worm in my bowl of cornflakes. I had gotten halfway through my breakfast before I discovered Roy's "gift."

I pushed open the door of Café Luna. The first thing I noticed was an enormous mobile—made up of moons and stars—suspended from the ceiling. The mobile reminded me of Natalie's passion for astrology. I wondered just how serious about that stuff she was.

Personally, I couldn't imagine trying to run my life according to the stars. How did a person account for events that were totally unpredictable—such as falling in love?

I spotted Natalie and Jayne sitting at a corner table. Natalie looked fantastic, as usual. This morning she was wearing tight black leggings and a cinnamon-colored shirt.

Natalie and Jayne seemed totally absorbed in their conversation. Natalie was leaning across the table, her face serious. As she spoke she gestured repeatedly with one arm. Jayne was listening and nodding, her eyes on Natalie's face. Neither of them had noticed my presence. I wondered if Natalie was giving Jayne advice about pursuing a possible relationship with John.

"I hear the coffee's pretty good here," I said as I approached the table. I expected Natalie to look up and smile.

Instead, Natalie jumped as if I had stuck her with a giant pin. Before I could say anything else, she grabbed her jacket from the back of her chair.

"I've got to go," she said shortly. Without

another word, Natalie headed for the door of Café Luna.

I felt paralyzed. Exactly what was going on? I stared at Natalie's retreating back, trying not to let my mouth hang open. Did I have a huge zit on my nose? Had I grown a third arm? What?

"What's up with Natalie?" I asked Jayne as soon as my voice would function. Jayne bit her lip. For a moment she stared into her cup of coffee. When she glanced up, her eyes were sympathetic.

"She's kind of upset right now," Jayne answered.

"No kidding," I said. I knew my voice sounded a little more sarcastic than I had intended it to. Natalie's sudden departure had left a funny feeling in the pit of my stomach. "Do you know what's going on?"

"I think Natalie should tell you herself," Jayne answered. "It's just—" Her blue eyes lifted to my face. "Try to give her some space, okay, Dean? I'm sure everything will work out once she's calmed down a little."

I was dying to pump Jayne for information. But before I could coax anything out of her, she stood up. Moments later she was gone.

I retreated to the counter and ordered a triple-shot grande latte. I hoped the extra caffeine would numb me. Until I could discover why Natalie was so upset, I would need all the help I could get.

"She's avoiding me," I said.

John and I were sitting in the Emerald High cafeteria, force-feeding ourselves portions of tuna surprise. I think the surprise had to do with the fact that we had gotten suckered into eating the stuff.

Natalie and Jayne were sitting at a nearby table. Natalie hadn't said a word to me all day. She hadn't even sat next to me in Mr. Dixon's English class. All day I had tried to take Jayne's advice. I was giving Natalie "space." But the more space I gave her, the more she avoided me.

"I just don't get it," I continued. "Yesterday afternoon we were kissing under her oak tree. Today she's treating me like I have the bubonic plague. Why?"

"Bad breath?" John suggested.

I sighed heavily. "This is serious, John."

A couple of sophomore girls at the table next to us started to giggle. *Great,* I thought. *They probably heard every single word.* I could already hear the rumors. *Natalie Taylor thinks Dean Smith has lice. Dean Smith begged Natalie for a second date—she told him she wouldn't go out with him if he were the last eligible guy on the planet.*

Ugh! For the sake of self-preservation, I had to find out what was going on.

I stabbed my fork into something that resembled green salad. I put the so-called lettuce into my mouth, chewed, and swallowed. The salad tasted like binder paper with Italian dressing. This day sucked.

If the way Natalie had avoided me all morning was any indication, she intended to go on pretending I wasn't alive for the rest of the day. Clearly I needed to take action.

"I'll be right back," I told John.

I walked the short distance to Natalie's table. Once again she and Jayne were deep in conversation. But this time I wasn't naive enough to think they were talking about John. I was positive they were discussing me—or more accurately, Natalie's sudden dislike of me.

"Natalie, can we talk?" I said, slipping into the chair next to hers.

Natalie's brown eyes looked enormous. There were big circles under them, as if she hadn't gotten any sleep last night. I could feel my stomach start to tense up. Something really serious was going on.

"Dean," Natalie said, her voice coming out all husky. "I'm, um, kind of talking to Jayne right now."

"Oh, that's all right," Jayne said, standing up quickly. "There's something I need to look up in the library anyway." She grabbed her tray from the table.

"Good luck," Jayne told me. The words sounded ominous. Then she race-walked toward the door of the cafeteria. Out of the corner of my eye I saw John get up and follow her.

A panicked expression crossed Natalie's face. "So," she squeaked. "How are you doing, Dean?"

Now I *knew* I was in trouble. Natalie was making polite conversation, a classic avoidance technique. I'd learned that pleasant chatter is the kiss of death in dating 101.

My frustration was building. I can't stand it when people don't tell me straight out what's on their minds. Natalie was the last person I would expect to play games with me.

"Why don't you *tell* me how I'm doing," I answered. "Until this morning, I thought I was doing fine. Great, actually." My voice had become louder as I spoke. I was almost shouting.

Natalie winced. "Please," she said. "I don't want to fight, Dean."

"I don't want to fight either," I said, more softly. "I just want you to tell me what's going on. If I've done something wrong, I think I have the right to know about it."

"No," Natalie whispered. "You haven't done anything wrong, Dean. It's just—I'm sorry. I can't see you anymore."

I felt as if Natalie had just picked up her chair and hit me over the head with it. Then denial set in. I must have misunderstood her. It was *not* possible that the girl of my dreams had just informed me that she didn't want to go out with me anymore.

"Let me see if I've got this straight," I said, my words slow and deliberate. "You're breaking up with me—but I haven't done anything wrong?"

Natalie didn't answer. She just nodded, her face pale.

"Well, that didn't take long," I said. "What have you been doing, taking lessons from Garth Hunter?"

Natalie's face turned dark pink. "I'm going to ignore your last comment," she said icily. "This isn't any easier for me than it is for you, Dean. I'm just trying to do what I think is right for both of us. Things would never have worked out between us."

I cleared my throat, which felt as if it were stuffed with cotton. "May I ask why you're so sure that things wouldn't work out?" I asked.

"You're the wrong astrological sign," Natalie said simply.

I began to reconsider the wisdom of the triple-shot grande I had earlier. Maybe I had so much caffeine in my system, I was going out of my mind.

"That's why you're breaking up with me?" I shouted. "Because I'm the wrong astrological sign?"

Natalie nodded. "I can't see you anymore because you're a Gemini. The sign is a really bad match for me."

"This is a joke," I insisted. "Please tell me this is a joke."

Natalie shook her head. "I know from experience that Geminis are bad news." She lowered her eyes to the tabletop. "Garth was a Gemini."

My stomach stopped churning—it now felt like a ball of lead. "This is all because of Garth, isn't it?" I asked, my voice flat. "Because you're still in love with him."

"I'm not," Natalie insisted. "I got over him a long time ago. It's just that Scorpios and Geminis don't mix. We're incompatible signs."

"Save it, Natalie."

Natalie put her hand on my arm. "I'm doing this for you too, Dean," she continued. "To keep you from being unhappy later."

"Well, that's really thoughtful of you," I said, jerking away my arm. "Instead I get to be unhappy now."

Natalie stood up. "I don't think I can talk to you about this anymore," she said. "I'm trying to explain, but you're not listening to me. You're deliberately trying to misunderstand." She stuffed the brown bag lunch she'd brought to school into her backpack.

"You're wrong," I said. "I do understand. I understand you're walking away from me for no reason."

"I have a reason," Natalie retorted. "You just don't want to accept it. I'm not going to stand here and argue with you. I never meant to hurt you. But I've said everything I have to say."

Before I could think of a way to stop her, she picked up her backpack and strode away. I was left standing in the middle of the lunchroom.

I must have just set a new world's record, I thought as I watched her push open the door. I had found, then managed to lose, a perfect relationship in exactly three and a half days.

The rest of the day was a total disaster. By the time I got to last-period P.E. class, I was ready to punch my fist through a wall. A very hard wall.

Every time I walked into a room, conversation stopped. The scene between Natalie and me at lunch was being discussed by the entire school. By Friday morning our breakup would probably be a headline in the school newspaper.

I spun the combination of my locker, purpose-fully ignoring the curious glances of the other guys in the locker room. I ripped off my jacket, then tossed it into my locker. Despite the cold weather, I couldn't wait to get outside. Running around the track was always a good outlet for frustration. And the sooner I got Natalie out of my system, the better.

I heard a burst of noise as the locker-room doors opened behind me. "Hey, Romeo," a voice called. "Got some love life problems?"

Oh, great, I thought. *Just what I need.*

I had wondered how long it would be before I encountered Garth Hunter. Garth has one of the most enormous egos on the planet. I was sure he wouldn't resist the opportunity to torture me.

I turned to face him. "Did you say something to me?"

The sight of Garth made me want to puke. I prayed that my tuna surprise would stay in my stomach. Throwing up in the locker room is hardly a show of masculinity.

How can she think he's a better guy than I am? I wondered as I looked at his smug expression. *He's a pig.*

"Yeah," Garth said. "I said too bad about you and Natalie." His blue eyes were sharp as he waited for my reaction. But I wasn't about to give him any more ammunition.

"Yeah," I said. "Too bad." I sat down on the bench and started to lace up my running shoes. I hoped Garth would let the subject drop. I should have known better.

"How long did it take her to unload you?" Garth asked. "All of about twenty minutes?"

"I wasn't counting," I said. "But I think she was trying to beat your world's record."

I could hear muffled laughter coming from the other side of the lockers. Most guys didn't like Garth any more than I did. He was popular through what John called the intimidation factor. It was easier to go along with him than to fight him.

"Hey, that's cute, Dean," Garth said, as if I'd given him a compliment. "Listen, I wouldn't take Natalie dumping you too hard. She couldn't help herself. She never really got over me."

"I guess you two have something in common," I said. "You're both in love with *you*."

Someone laughed out loud on the far side of the

locker room. Garth scowled as he took off his letterman's jacket.

"Well, you can't blame us," Garth said finally. "I'm pretty outstanding." He grinned. "And Natalie's not the only girl in school who can't stop fantasizing about me."

I was wrong about you, Garth, I thought. *You don't have the biggest ego on the planet. You have the biggest ego in the solar system.*

"So let me get this straight. You're saying Natalie would rather *dream* about you than *date* me?"

Garth smiled, revealing years' worth of expensive orthodontics. "I guess we'll never know now, will we?"

Big mistake, I said silently. Garth Hunter had just dared me.

His words might have been intended to make me recognize the hopelessness of my situation. But they had the opposite effect on me. I felt better than I had since Natalie had dissed me at Café Luna.

There was a way to prove I was better than Garth Hunter. All I had to do was to convince Natalie to get back together with me. Which was all I really wanted in the first place.

Five

NATALIE

Scorpio (Oct. 23–Nov. 21)
Fortunes crash as your heart battles with
your head. Try stepping back from the situation.
Let things ride. You're called upon to assist one
who always assists you. Remember the healing
properties of time.

"I DON'T SEE what you're so upset about," I said
to Jayne Friday afternoon. "You're not the
one who had to give up her boyfriend."

"No," Jayne agreed glumly. "Just my only possibility of ever getting one."

We were sitting at a table by the front window
of the Seattle Dessert Company, drowning our sorrows in huge bowls of double chocolate decadence
ice cream. Sometimes affairs of the heart take
precedence over affairs of the figure.

Dean hadn't spoken to me since our blowup in
the cafeteria on Tuesday.

I had told myself a thousand times that I should be glad Dean hadn't tried to talk me out of breaking up. I really had said everything there was to say. And Dean hadn't understood the astrological reasons for our breakup. In fact, he had reacted with hostility to the whole topic of astrology.

Of course, I had to admit to myself that not everyone in the world was as enlightened about astrology as I was. Not even Jayne understood why reading the stars was so important to me.

Sure, I knew that I had made the right decision. But being misunderstood was painful. Overall, I had never felt worse in my life.

Now that I couldn't look forward to seeing Dean, I realized how long he had been a part of my life. For the entire school year I had been acutely aware of his presence. Now his absence was creating a romantic vacuum that my Scorpio nature found difficult to deal with. I was in total gridlock.

Naturally I turned to Jayne for consolation. I had even contemplated that the short-term solution to my situation might be to take a more Pisces-like approach to life. I should step back, consider my actions, be ruled by my head.

But Jayne wasn't helping. She was about as cheerful as a tax accountant. If the amount of ice cream she was eating was any indication, Jayne was just as depressed as I was.

"What do you mean your only possibility of ever getting a boyfriend?" I asked. I let her know by the tone of my voice that I wasn't feeling overly sympathetic. We weren't here to drown *her* sorrows in expensive, high-calorie chocolate. We were here to drown *mine*.

Jayne stabbed her spoon into her bowl of double chocolate decadence. "You ought to remember," she said. "You said it yourself. I'm your best friend. John is Dean's. It was the perfect setup for us to get to know each other. Now that you and Dean aren't together, John and I have, like, no chance."

I stared at her. "You mean you really *do* like John Muirhead?"

I had suspected that Jayne had a crush on John when we had all been at Bob's Buzz Stop last weekend. But since then, she hadn't even mentioned him.

"Of course I do," Jayne said. "I've liked him for months. I can't believe you couldn't tell."

"I guess I've been so upset about what happened with Dean that I forgot all about you and John."

Jayne ate another spoonful of double chocolate decadence. "That's okay," she said. "I mean, it's not like we should waste any more time talking about this. John will probably never even look at me again." She sighed.

I suddenly realized how selfish I had been all week. After all, Jayne was my best friend. I shouldn't abandon the cause of her love live just because mine was hopeless.

"Well, we'll just have to make sure he *does* look, Jayne."

Jayne's spoon froze midair. "What do you mean?"

"I mean you shouldn't give up. If you really like him, you should let him know it."

"But how?" Jayne said. "Without you and Dean—"

"The relationship you should focus on is the one between you and John," I said firmly. "Not the one between me and Dean. Just because we're history doesn't mean you guys have to be."

"But I don't see how it could work," Jayne protested.

"We need a plan," I announced.

I reached under my chair and pulled out my backpack. "You and John Muirhead *will* be a couple." I unzipped my backpack and rummaged for a ballpoint pen. Then I opened my notebook to a clean page.

Already I was starting to feel much better. Helping Jayne and John get together would be the perfect outlet for my thwarted romantic Scorpio tendencies.

"This planning session is hereby called to order," I said. I made a column with Jayne's name at the top of one side of the paper. On the other side I did the same for John.

"All right, let's start with the basics," I instructed. "We'll make a list of things you guys have in common. Then we'll cross-reference them to figure out if any of them translate into dating opportunities."

"I can't believe you're actually going to do this," Jayne said. But I noticed she had stopped eating. "Is this how the really popular girls do things?"

"The *really* popular girls have computer databases," I answered. "But we have to make do with the technology at hand. Now, what's the first thing you and John have in common?"

Jayne thought about it for a moment. "You and Dean?"

"How about totally unbelievable grade point averages? And being on the honor roll," I countered. "Those things will probably get us further. Now, what else?"

"We both drink mochas?"

"Excellent," I said. "Now we're really starting to get somewhere."

Half an hour later my mood had improved enormously. I had even laughed a couple of times. I had filled both sides of the paper. The most likely cross-references for John and Jayne getting to know each other better were caffeine consumption and the chess club. We'd also decided that Jayne should try to sit next to John in English as much as possible, even if it meant she and I didn't sit together. And that she should loiter by John's locker for five minutes at least once a day.

"So we're set," I said to Jayne. I ripped out the sheet of notebook paper I had been writing on and handed it to Jayne. "Guard this with your life," I told her.

She folded up the piece of paper and stuck it into the back pocket of her Levi's. "Don't worry; I will. Can you imagine how humiliated I'd be if anyone found this list?"

I laughed. "Don't even think it."

I zipped up my backpack and stood up. As I followed Jayne out of the restaurant I forced myself to admit the truth.

The fact that I was helping my best friend find true love wasn't the only reason I was feeling better. I also knew that no matter what had happened between Dean and me, Dean was still John's best friend.

And helping Jayne and John get together was the perfect excuse for me to stay close to Dean.

"Natalie, a package came for you," my mom called the second I walked in the door.

60

"Really?" I asked. Hmmm. Who could be sending me a package? I had finally ended my subscription to Columbia House Records after years of being harassed via the post office.

I cut through the living room and joined my mother in the kitchen. She was standing at the stove, stirring a big pot of something that smelled incredibly good.

"What is it?" I asked her, going to peer over her shoulder.

"Chili," my mother answered. "And salad and corn bread, if you can believe it. I got off work early because there was a power outage in our building."

"Great! A real dinner!"

My mom grinned. "Don't tell me you're tired of Pizza Hut and Taco Bell?"

"Never," I answered. "Now where's that package?"

"On the table, sweetheart."

We always put the mail in a basket on the kitchen table. That way, nothing gets lost. Today's mail consisted of a small box of sample laundry detergent, one of my father's endless computer magazines, and a Lands' End catalog. Next to the basket was a brown paper package with my name on the front.

Ms. Natalie Taylor
3609 Seaview Street
Seattle, WA 98199

My heart began to beat a little faster. I was almost certain the bold, black handwriting belonged to Dean.

I flipped over the package. There was no return

61

address. I could practically *feel* my mom's curious stare.

"Who's it from?" she asked.

I hadn't talked to my mom much about my recent love life fiasco. But since she's loaded with maternal intuition, I had the feeling she knew there was something going on. Even so, I decided against revealing that there was a very good chance the mystery package was from the guy I'd just had to break up with. My mom doesn't always understand my commitment to the stars.

I shrugged. "I don't know. There's no return address."

"Ah, a secret admirer," my mom commented.

I rolled my eyes. "Get a life, Mom."

My mother began to gather the ingredients for the corn bread.

"What's the magic word?" she asked.

"Please," I said. "Please get a life."

"And they say young people today have no manners."

I tucked the package under my arm. This conversation was going nowhere. "I'm going upstairs to open this. See you in a little while."

"When you're done, it would help if you could set the table."

"Okay, Mom." *As long as I'm not sobbing too much to come downstairs,* I added silently.

My bedroom is on the second floor of our house. Right outside my window are the branches of the tree Dean and I had been standing under the last time we had kissed.

Once I was in the safety of my bedroom, it took me a couple of minutes to get up my courage to open Dean's package. At least the parcel wasn't ticking. I ruled out the possibility that he had mailed me a homemade pipe bomb.

Stop being such a chicken, Natalie. Dean isn't the type to send hate mail.

I got a pair of scissors from my desk. Carefully I sliced through the brown paper. When I pulled off the paper, I saw that an object was carefully wrapped in several layers of newspaper. I tore through the newspaper. By now I was about to explode from curiosity.

At last I saw a picture frame. The frame looked almost antique. It was made of polished wood and decorated with a raised border of gilded roses. Inside the frame was a picture of me and Dean. A lump formed in my throat as I stared down at the photograph.

The picture was the one the photographer had taken of us at the Sweethearts' Dance on Valentine's Day.

Dean and I were staring at the camera and smiling. The color of the red rose arch above our heads was a perfect match for my corsage. Our huge grins radiated happiness.

Only forty-eight hours after that photo was snapped, Dean and I had faced each other in the Emerald High cafeteria. And I had broken up with him.

I flopped onto my bed and cradled the picture against my chest. I could still remember how I had felt when Dean and I had been standing in front of that goofy photographer. At that moment I never would have guessed that Dean and I weren't meant to last. Everything had seemed so perfect.

I closed my eyes. In my mind Dean and I were out on the dance floor, slowly swaying to the music. When we slow-danced, I totally forgot that other people were out on the gym floor. My whole body had started to tingle as I'd sensed that Dean was about to kiss me.

Later I rested my head on his shoulder as we drove toward my house after the dance. I had felt wonderful and romantic, like a glamorous woman out of an old black-and-white movie.

My brain told me that ending things with Dean had been the right thing to do. Our signs were completely incompatible. I had learned that the hard way. I knew that getting involved with another Gemini would put me on a disastrous course. I would be setting myself up for heartbreak.

Unfortunately my heart was feeling pretty broken right this moment. I would have given anything to feel once again like the girl in that picture frame. The girl who thought the future was going to be bright and rosy.

Natalie, you're the ultimate sap, I thought, staring down at the picture. Sometimes I had the bad habit of thinking about life in terms of a Hallmark card.

You know what you've got to do, I told myself. The only way to get over Dean was to put him behind me once and for all. I simply couldn't afford to get all sentimental over this picture. I needed to treat the photograph as ruthlessly as I did all those pictures of Garth.

I tried to imagine destroying Dean's gift. Sneaking downstairs in the middle of the night. I saw myself opening the lid of the garbage and tossing in the beautiful frame.

But I knew I could never do it. Not in a million years.

I could never destroy a picture of the two of us together—even if I was asking for trouble by dwelling in the past. Dean had meant too much to me. Maybe he still meant too much.

I set the frame on my nightstand. Dean's smiling face would be the last thing I saw at night and the first thing I saw in the morning.

Six

Dean

Gemini (May 21–June 20)
Determination! If life has dealt you some low blows lately, now is the time to show what you're made of. Your desire to prove yourself could lead you down a blind alley. Keep your eyes (and your heart) open.

"OKAY," I SAID to John. "So much for phase one. Which, if I may say so myself, was absolutely brilliant."

It was Saturday morning, and we were sitting in our favorite corner booth at Burger Palace.

John lifted his chocolate shake in a salute. "Phase one. That was the picture, right?"

"Of course it was the picture. Haven't you been paying attention, John?"

My plan to convince Natalie we should get back together was progressing. I had been psyched when the photograph from the Sweethearts' Dance had arrived in the mail. Sending Natalie the picture was the perfect way to start my campaign.

But seeing documented evidence of how happy Natalie and I were then had been upsetting. Our relationship had such a promising beginning. But the whole thing had come crashing down almost as soon as it started.

I hoped that giving Natalie our picture would make her think of all the good things about our being together. Maybe she'd even start to miss me a little. But I couldn't rely on a photograph to do all my work. There had to be other ways of proving to her that we should get back together.

"What do you think of all this astrology business?" I asked John.

John took a sip of mocha. Today his hair looked as though it had been through a blender. "I don't know, Dean," he answered. "Natalie's obsession with the stars seems pretty wacky to me."

"Tell me about it," I said. "I can't believe she's serious."

John was silent for a moment. "She certainly sounded serious about it. I mean, it's the whole reason she broke up with you, right?"

"She broke up with me because of Garth Hunter," I answered.

"Because you and Garth are both whatchamacallits."

"Geminis. But that has to be an excuse. That can't be her real reason. It doesn't make any sense."

"Dean," John said. "We're talking about a *girl*. Girls rarely make sense."

I grinned at him across the table. John did have a point. There was only so far a guy could go when it came to understanding the workings of the female mind. "So what do you suggest?" I asked.

"Well, you and I know this astrology stuff is totally bogus," John said thoughtfully. "But we shouldn't assume that Natalie knows it. Girls just don't think the way we do. Besides, we do have pretty strong evidence that astrology is really important to Natalie."

"Such as?" I asked.

"That day we ran into Natalie and Jayne having coffee, the first thing Natalie did was to ask me my sign," he reminded me.

"You're right," I said, drumming my fingers on the table. At the time I had assumed that her astrology question was just a way to get the conversation rolling. But now . . . "So a smart guy would go for the astrology angle, or at least he wouldn't ignore it."

"That's right," John agreed. "But we don't have to become believers. We can use the scientific method. Gather information. See where it leads us."

"This is good," I said. "I like this, John. Now all we have to do is to figure out where to get information about astrology."

John pointed to a flyer posted on the wall of Bob's Buzz Stop. "How about a New Age store?"

Two hours later I staggered away from the checkout counter at Everything Under the Sun Books. In my arms I held every single book I had found about the astrological sign of Gemini.

I'd skimmed through a few of the books while I was standing in line: *Under the Stars, Knowing Your Zodiac Sign, Better Life Through Astrology.*

Unfortunately the material I had located wasn't very encouraging. I had to admit that I could sort of see why Natalie had reached the conclusion that she didn't want to get involved with another Gemini.

The list of Gemini attributes conjured up an almost exact profile of Garth Hunter. Charming and dynamic were right up there on top of the list. But those adjectives were followed immediately by flighty, fickle, and unpredictable.

Still, I wasn't going to be discouraged. I wasn't about to be done in by my own sign. If I learned what kind of personality a Gemini was supposed to have, I would be in the perfect position to prove to Natalie that I had nothing in common with fellow members of my sign.

"Hey," John called, clutching a book titled *Love Signs of the Zodiac* to his chest. "Check that out." He waved toward the front window of the store.

"Madame Sonya's House of Fortune," I read aloud from the sign near the entrance of the bookstore that John was pointing to. "Palm Reader. Fortune-teller. Interpreter of the Tarot. Let Madame Sonya Show You the Way."

"A visit to Madame Sonya might be just what you need," John said. "A secret weapon."

"Absolutely not," I answered. "I am not going to a fortune-teller, John."

John shrugged. "Don't be so narrow-minded. She might tell you something you want to hear. If nothing else, you could sort of casually work your visit into a conversation with Natalie. It would probably really impress her to know you were serious enough about getting her back that you actually acquired a spiritual adviser."

John was right, of course. He usually is. We walked out of the bookstore. By tacit agreement we headed toward Madame Sonya's.

But I still wasn't sure I was ready to have my fortune told. I hesitated outside the entrance of Madame Sonya's shop. A beaded curtain hung across the door. The musky smell of incense wafted through the air.

I hate incense. Just the thought of the stuff makes my sinuses revolt. I felt the urge to sneeze.

"I can't do it, John," I said. "Smell that. If I go inside, I'll be washing incense out of my hair for a week."

"Okay," John said, turning from the shop. "If you're scared, I totally understand."

"Oh, no, you don't," I told him. "You can't make me go through with this just because you've turned it into a dare."

John nodded. "You're absolutely right," he said. "It was a low blow, and I apologize. You're obviously way too adult to succumb to such a sneaky, underhanded trick. And besides, it probably won't help you get Natalie back anyway."

"You just said you thought it would," I contradicted.

John shrugged again. "So maybe I made a mistake. I'm not a spiritual adviser. I can't be right all the time, Dean."

I hate reverse psychology—especially because it always works on me. "Fine. I'll go," I said. "But I'm not going in there alone. If she tells my fortune, she tells yours too."

John tightened his grip on *Love Signs of the Zodiac.* "Paranormal research," he said. "This is going to be excellent."

I sneezed the second I walked into Madame Sonya's House of Fortune. There was an incense burner right by the door. Another curtain-covered doorway was straight ahead of us. I figured the beads led to Madame Sonya's inner sanctum.

I gazed around the room in which we were standing now. The walls were draped in dark fabric. On the ceiling there was gauzy fabric, which was speckled with sparkling dots. I assumed the sparkles were meant to represent the stars. Speakers above our heads emitted soulful gypsy violin music. I felt a momentary flare of hope. Maybe Madame Sonya was going to turn out to be young and beautiful, like Esmerelda in *The Hunchback of Notre Dame.* Maybe her very presence would make me forget that Natalie Taylor existed.

No such luck. Madame Sonya emerged from behind the beaded curtain. She was wearing an elaborate turban on her head, and she looked as if she had cornered the market on purple eye shadow. Her face was caked with heavy makeup.

"Ah, two young unbelievers," she said, her voice thick with some unidentifiable accent. She sounded a bit like Count Dracula.

"You have come to consult Madame Sonya about your miserable love lives, have you not?" she asked. Her black eyes glittered.

Beside me John coughed. I assumed he was try-ing not to laugh.

"Madame Sonya, we're desperate," John said after another cough. "You've got to help us."

Madame Sonya smiled. Her teeth were very white and very pointed. Maybe she really was a vampire. "Madame Sonya will help you. Don't you worry," the fortune-teller replied. She moved aside and gestured for us to precede her. "Step inside."

"Tell his fortune first," I instructed Madame Sonya several minutes later. I pointed at John.

We had reached the inner sanctum of the House of Fortune. John and I were seated in a pair of uncomfortable folding chairs. Across the table Madame Sonya was lounging on an overstuffed red velvet settee.

I suspected that Madame Sonya had selected the uncomfortable chairs on purpose. She probably wanted her customers to pay more attention to their butts going to sleep than to her pseudopsychic readings.

Madame Sonya frowned. "You must learn patience," she told me. "You are a very impatient young man." Her accent had gotten thicker now that we were into the actual fortune-telling session.

"Hey, we're supposed to be talking about John," I said.

She rolled her eyes. "Fine, fine. I vill start with your friend, zince zou request it."

Madame Sonya stretched her arm out on the table. "Show to me your palm."

John inched his arm forward. Madame Sonya seized his hand. She lifted his palm to just under her nose. My own nose began to itch; I felt like I was about to sneeze again. For John's sake I hoped incense didn't have the same effect on Madame Sonya.

"You are zeeking zomething," Madame Sonya murmured. "You are zeeking your own true love. She is very cloze. Zo cloze, maybe you do not see her. It is not alvays easy to recognize a mate of the soul."

This is great, I thought. *Soul mate. Mate of the soul.* Madame Sonya had just given me the perfect opportunity to torture John.

"Hey, John," I whispered loudly. "She's talking about Jayne Engerman."

John refused to look at me. He kept all his attention focused on the fortune-teller. "Dean, be quiet. You're disturbing the spiritual vibrations."

"But she has to be talking about Jayne," I insisted. "Natalie said you two were soul mates."

"You go to another fortune-teller?" Madame Sonya demanded. "Who is she, this Natalie?"

"She's the girl *he's* in love with," John answered.

"Just like you're in love with Jayne," I said.

"Oh, all right," John said, pulling his hand back across the table. "You want me to admit it? I admit it. I like Jayne Engerman."

"Good," I said. "Now maybe you can *do* something about it."

"Can we move on to your fortune, please?" John asked. Even in the dim light I could see that he was blushing. "You're the one who needed help in the first place."

Madame Sonya shook her head. She stared briefly at each of us. "Much conflict," she murmured. "There is too much conflict in this room. It is bad for the reading. It clouds the spirit."

She glared at me from across the table. "Your palm. You vill give it to me."

Slowly I extended my palm toward Madame Sonya. The situation didn't seem quite so amusing now that she was about to focus her psychic powers on me.

Madame Sonya grabbed my hand. She ran her pointed scarlet-colored fingernails across the palm. "Ah," she said, as if she had discovered something important. "Zo this is vere the conflict comes. You are very unhappy. Very unhappy in love. You make miserable everyone around you."

Brilliant deduction, I thought. Any idiot could have figured that out. Besides, whoever heard of happy people consulting a fortune-teller? Fortune-tellers were like therapists—people only went to see them when there was something wrong.

"Your path is very rocky," Madame Sonya went on. "Much more rocky than that for your friend. He has but to open his eyes and look around him. Your eyes, they are already open. But your mind is filled with delusions. You zee only vhat you vish to zee."

At the moment I didn't want to see anything but daylight. Madame Sonya was giving me the creeps.

Abruptly the fortune-teller sat up straight. She lifted my palm up high above her head.

"You are on the right path, but you hold cloze to your heart the thing which is preventing your happiness. You must release it. *Release it!*" Madame Sonya shook my arm so hard that I thought she might have pulled it out of its socket. "Then your love vill fly free!"

She let go of my hand. Then she sat back, as if

the session had been spiritually exhausting.

"That is all that I can tell you," Madame Sonya continued. "The spiritual impressions, they have left me."

"Well, uh, thanks," John said. He stood up. He seemed as anxious to leave as I was.

"That will be twenty dollars apiece," Madame Sonya informed us. "I give you good bargain. Come back and see me again sometime. Have a nice day."

I reached for my wallet. Twenty bucks for five minutes of mumbo jumbo. Maybe I would scratch worrying about SATs and take up fortune-telling for a living.

"Well, that was spiritually illuminating," I said as John and I walked through the beaded curtain. "My whole future is crystal clear to me."

"You've got to admit, it was an interesting experience," John said.

"Interesting, yes," I said. "But worth twenty bucks? No."

As we headed toward John's car I pondered Madame Sonya's words. Maybe she was right. Maybe I was delusional. Delusion number one? That I had any chance, whatsoever, to win Natalie back.

Monday morning I slid into my seat just as the last bell rang. A moment later I felt someone's eyes on me. Could it be? I held my breath and said a quick prayer.

I glanced sideways. Natalie was staring straight at me. My heart skipped a beat. She looked away immediately. She was probably hoping I hadn't noticed her looking at me.

But I was happy. This was the first time since we had broken up that she had looked directly at me. Sending the photograph had been a good move. I was gaining ground. Correction—I wasn't *losing* ground.

I opened my notebook as Dufus Dixon started his lecture. We were almost to the end of *Romeo and Juliet*. By this act in the play half of the important characters were dead. The other half were making such stupid mistakes that there was little doubt that they were doomed as well. The Montagues and Capulets were two families who would have definitely benefited from some family counseling.

I realized I was the only person in the classroom who was staring at a blank sheet of paper. Everyone else was studying their copy of *Romeo and Juliet*. Quickly I opened my book. I pretended to pay attention to Mr. Dixon's lecture. But all I could think about was Natalie. I needed to plan my next move.

I didn't think I should go right up and ask her how she had liked the picture. The situation seemed to call for a more indirect approach. Something with finesse. Something that would let her know I cared but wouldn't make me seem too eager. There was no sense in totally sacrificing what was left of my male ego.

I kept my eye on Mr. Dixon while I considered my options. The Dufus was marching around in front of the classroom, trailing huge clouds of chalk dust.

Mr. Dixon turned around abruptly, his back to the classroom. He began scribbling furiously on the chalkboard. An ideal opportunity had arisen. I would use these moments of freedom to write Natalie a note.

In my experience girls were always writing notes to one another. But they rarely received notes from the male half of the species. I couldn't, for example, imagine Garth Hunter taking the time to send a love letter—or anything else—to the girl of his dreams.

Perfect, I thought. *Totally* un-*Gemini.*

I uncapped my pen. I hoped that if Dufus Dixon caught sight of me writing, he would assume I was taking notes on his incredibly memorable lecture.

"Dear Natalie," I wrote.

> Did you get the picture that I sent? When I look at that photograph, I get total recall. I can almost hear the tape with those stupid bird sounds on it.

Okay. Now what? I had no idea what to say next. I couldn't come right out and *beg.* Or could I?

> Anyway, I really hope you like it as much as I do. Maybe we could go out for coffee sometime at your favorite spot, Café Luna. If so, just say the word. You know where to find me. I'm the guy at the end of the row—trying to stay awake during this totally boring lecture.
> I miss you,
> Dean

The note was a little dorky. The sentiment was a cross between something I would write in a yearbook and the kind of letter I used to send to my mother from summer camp. But at least I hadn't told her to "stay cute as always and have a good time with the guys this summer."

I folded the note in half and wrote Natalie's name across the front of it. I forced myself to hand the note to John before I could change my mind.

"Pass this down," I whispered, careful to keep my eyes on Mr. Dixon. The last time he had caught somebody passing a note, he had made her write its contents on the chalkboard fifty times.

John passed the note to Becky Greer, who was sitting next to him. Becky passed the note to Gretchen Rubin.

I shut my eyes. The note was out of my hands. Now I just had to wait for Natalie's reaction.

Seven

NATALIE

Scorpio (Oct. 23–Nov. 21)

Battle of the sexes continues. There will be
moments when you feel besieged. Hope may lie
in a surprise revelation. Practice random acts
of selfless kindness, better known as good deeds.

"NATALIE," JAYNE WHISPERED loudly.

I jumped. I had been zoning out on
Mr. Dixon's lecture about the relative merits of
Juliet's two suitors, Paris and Romeo.

It was hardly the most fascinating way to begin a
Monday morning. And discussing Paris was a total
waste of time. No girl in her right mind was ever
going to fall in love with a guy who had been
picked out by her father.

"What?" I whispered in Jayne's general direction. I kept both eyes fixed on Mr. Dixon. I couldn't
afford to get caught talking in class a second time.

Jayne didn't answer me. Instead she slid a folded piece of notebook paper onto my desk. My name was written in capital letters across the front of it. For the second time I recognized the handwriting. It was Dean's.

Dean had sent me a note. He had more courage than I would have guessed—Dean knew that if Mr. Dixon found the note, its contents would end up all over the blackboard.

All weekend long I had tried to think about what approach to take when I saw Dean on Monday morning. I had to acknowledge the fact that he had sent me the picture of the two of us together. I couldn't just ignore it. . . .

Finally I had resolved to be friendly, but aloof. I would thank Dean politely for the gift. But I wouldn't thank him so warmly that he could think I wanted to get back together.

There was only one problem. I was going to have to talk to Dean. We hadn't said a word to each other since that horrible day in the cafeteria. Just the thought of looking in his eyes and speaking made my heart beat a thousand times a second.

I had promised myself last night that I would get the "thank you" over with first thing Monday morning. But as soon as Dean had walked into English, I had known I was never going to be able to go through with my adult, mature plan. When I'd been lying in bed, imagining the cool, calm way I would graciously thank Dean for the photo, the scenario had seemed totally plausible. But in my mind I had left out one very important element of what the situation would be. My feelings.

I wasn't even sure what my feelings *were*, but I did know I hadn't reached a point where I could think of Dean as just a casual friend.

I put my hand on top of Dean's note. Maybe I could absorb its content through osmosis. Why had he written it? What did it say?

According to the attributes of his astrological sign, writing a note wasn't something Dean should have done at all. In my experience a Gemini always wanted to be the focus of attention. The Gemini in Dean should have been determined to wait for me to make the first move.

In fact, all Dean's behavior in relation to the photograph of us at the dance was totally un-Gemini. If I hadn't known better, I would have said he was acting like a pure Taurus.

The fact that Dean was behaving like a Taurus was extremely confusing. More than anything, I wanted to respond to him the way I always had. But I knew I couldn't afford to let myself do it.

I couldn't let it matter to me that Dean didn't *seem* like a Gemini. He was one. Sooner or later we were destined for disaster. The fact that we would crash and burn was written in the stars.

I glanced back down at the note. I couldn't wait a second longer. My fingers were aching to unfold the paper and see what was written inside.

I kept my eyes on Dufus Dixon as I opened the note and smoothed the paper. I scanned the sentences once, then twice. I folded the note back up and slid it safely underneath my notebook. My heart was pounding.

Maybe Dean has just done me a favor, I

thought. If I thanked him for the picture in a response note, we wouldn't have to talk.

I opened my notebook to a clean piece of paper. At the front of the classroom Mr. Dixon dropped a piece of chalk. As he bent over to pick up the chalk I started to write. . . .

> Dear Dean,
>   The picture was great. I really loved it. And I know just what you mean about those little birdie sounds. And every time I think of the crazy photographer who snapped the pic, I laugh.

I paused. *What am I doing?* I asked myself. *I can't send him a note that sounds like this.* My note wasn't friendly yet aloof. It was just plain friendly.

I crossed out everything I had written and started again.

> Dear Dean,
>   Thank you very much for the lovely picture. I particularly liked the frame. Did you have to look a long time to find one with roses on it?
>   Thanks again,
>   Natalie

Well, that's certainly a huge improvement, I thought sarcastically, staring down at the short note. I sounded as if I were in the second grade. The note was practically an exact replica of every thank-you letter I'd ever written to my grandmother. I crossed it out.

Come on, Natalie, I told myself. *You can do this. It isn't cancer research. It's just a thank-you note.*

Mr. Dixon was back at the blackboard. He was making a list of who was still alive from the houses of Montague and Capulet at this point in the play.

"Dear Dean," I wrote for the third and hopefully final time.

Your gift was very thoughtful. Thank you.

That was it. Just two sentences. Friendly, but aloof.

I tore the piece of paper out of my notebook. I folded it in half once, then twice. Quickly I wrote Dean's name across the front of the note and handed it to Jayne before I could change my mind.

I watched her hand it off to Kirk Parker out of the corner of my eye. Just as Kirk's hand closed around the small piece of paper my heart stopped. A cold numbness traveled the length of my spine.

I hadn't made a clean copy of the note. I had been so determined to get the note to Dean before the end of the period that I hadn't even thought to rewrite those two measly sentences on another sheet of paper. How could I have been so totally stupid?

Now Dean would know how hard I'd had to work to answer him. And he'd know all the things I'd been afraid to say.

"So," Jayne said. "Are you going to tell me what was in the note or what?"

We were sitting in Emerald High's somewhat dingy snack bar, drinking hot chocolate and trying not to give way to a lust for maple bars. We had another ten minutes before our midmorning break was over.

I still hadn't showed Dean's note to Jayne. I was finding myself reluctant to talk about the subject of Dean at all. Since English class I had been fighting off thoughts about Dean. But keeping my mind off him was impossible. The note had caused too many issues to rise to the surface.

I shrugged. "He just wanted to know if I liked a picture that he sent me, that's all."

"Was there anything about John and me?" Jayne asked.

"No, there wasn't," I said. For the millionth time in the last few weeks I felt guilty for forgetting that other people have as many emotions as I do. "I'm sorry, Jayne."

Jayne swirled a spoon around in her hot chocolate. "This business of trying to show John I like him. It's never going to work, is it, Natalie?"

"Of course it's going to work," I protested. "You can't give up yet. It's only Monday. The only thing you've had time to do so far is sit next to him in English."

"And I didn't even manage that," Jayne sighed.

"Tomorrow is another day," I insisted. "You'll sit next to him then."

"I know," Jayne answered. "It's just—I was really hoping Dean had said something. I mean, you guys don't really have your own relationship to talk about, so when I saw he'd written you a note, I thought maybe it was about John and me."

"I wish it had been," I said. *Then I wouldn't be feeling so totally confused right now,* I added silently.

"I think I'll go to the library," Jayne announced. "I have a book that's overdue."

Jayne never had overdue books, but I didn't see any reason to call her on it. She was obviously upset—I didn't want to intrude. "Okay," I said. "Don't forget: At lunchtime you've got locker duty."

"Yeah, right, for all the good it'll do." Jayne swung her book bag onto her shoulders and walked off. I continued to sit in the snack bar, gazing into the depths of my hot chocolate.

I'm not helping very much, I realized. Jayne was discouraged, and we hadn't even gotten through half of Monday. A girl more used to the dating scene would know not to expect miracles overnight. But Jayne was *not* familiar with the dating scene.

In my mind I went over the list that Jayne and I had made about what she and John had in common. Maybe there was something I had overlooked. Something that could give Jayne more immediate feedback. Even the most confident girl finds it difficult to go after a guy when she's not sure he's really interested.

I took another sip of hot chocolate. What we needed was a social occasion. An event that would throw Jayne and John together—and then force them to spend time with each other, preferably time that involved close bodily contact.

A dance would have been perfect. But there wasn't another dance until after spring break.

I tapped my spoon against the cup of hot chocolate. The next best thing to a dance would be a party. Parties usually involved slow dancing. But how could I be sure that John would ask Jayne to dance?

Come on, Natalie, I thought. *There has to be a solution. Think like Jayne would. Pretend you're a Pisces.*

I needed to be rational and logical. There had to be a way to make sure that both Jayne and John ended up in the same place at the same time. I could worry about the dancing and flirtatious conversation later.

A birthday party was the most obvious option. Jayne's birthday was coming up. If I threw a party for her and invited John to it—

"Natalie," I said out loud. "You are a complete and total idiot." I'd overlooked the most obvious thing that Jayne and John shared.

They had the same birthday. And although they didn't know it yet, Jayne and John were going to share a birthday party.

Eight

DEAN

Gemini (May 21–June 20)
Breakthrough! Things begin to move in your
direction, even though it may not be obvious
at first. Your dedication and perseverance
are your strongest assets. Don't let justifiable
anger allow you to get sidetracked.

"YOU CAN SO do it," I said. "Come on,
you've got to help me out here, John."

"I just don't see what good this is going to do,"
John protested.

We were standing in the hallway during
lunchtime. Down the corridor Jayne and Natalie
were standing right in front of John's locker.

"I told you," I said. "I want to know how
Natalie is feeling. But I still think it's a bad idea
to take the direct approach. Which means you
need to pump Jayne for information." I sighed.
"I don't see why you're making such a big deal

out of it. You know you want to talk to her."

A panicked expression crossed John's face. He looked more like he was about to face the firing squad than talk to a cute girl. Even his hair had gone limp with tension.

"Well, yeah, I want to talk to her," John admitted. "But I was thinking sometime in the distant future. Like maybe around the year 2000."

"The year 2000 will be too late, John." I paused. "Come on, I dare you."

"Forget it," he said. "You're the one who can't resist a dare. Not me."

"Look at it this way," I told him. "If you don't talk to her, you'll spend the rest of your life wondering what might have happened if you had. She's not going to wait for you forever. She'll find some other guy. Then you'll really feel stupid."

John groaned. "All right, all right, I'm going," he said. "But if this backfires, I'm going to teach your little brothers every science experiment I know that involves the use of smelly chemicals."

I laughed. "Good luck."

I watched as John walked down the hall toward Jayne and Natalie. I leaned against the row of lockers behind me and tried to look like I was thinking about something important. When John reached the girls, I noticed that Jayne's face turned sort of red. But Natalie just smiled. After a moment Jayne and John walked off.

At that moment I realized that having arranged for John and Jayne to be together had a consequence I hadn't considered. Natalie and I were now alone.

Well, we weren't exactly alone. We were standing in the middle of a crowded high-school hallway. And we weren't even standing next to each other. But it felt like we were all alone.

I told myself I should just walk over, kind of casually. Then I remembered that I had promised myself I wouldn't take the direct approach. Still, I wasn't sure I could resist this opportunity to talk to her.

Before I could weigh the pros and cons of talking to her versus not talking to her, Natalie made the decision for me. She looked in my direction. Then she smiled and gave me the thumbs-up sign. She actually took a couple of steps toward me. My heart leaped. Natalie was going to speak to me— voluntarily.

But when she was still several feet away, she froze in her tracks. Without looking at me again, Natalie turned and walked off down the hall.

I watched as she strolled all the way down the corridor. By the time I headed off to my next class, I was feeling pretty good.

Natalie was definitely giving me mixed signals. Which was better than no signals at all. Things were definitely starting to look up.

"Dean! Over here!" Frank Sebree yelled.

I threw the basketball to Frank, then wiped the sweat out of my eyes. I raced down the court in time to watch Peter Jackson make a perfect slam dunk. The other team took possession and tossed the ball in from the sidelines.

There was almost always a game of basketball

going on after school in the gym at the local community center. And today I had needed to expend some extra energy in a major way. After all the stuff that had happened with Natalie at school, I was feeling pretty hyped.

Peter passed me the basketball. I dribbled downcourt, then bounced the ball between the legs of an opposing player to a teammate. Once again we scored.

So far everything was going the way I wanted it to. I was making progress with Natalie. And I'd even managed to do a little work on John and Jayne. A couple more days of this and we could all live happily ever after. Maybe instead of fortune-telling I'd go into matchmaking.

"Hey, you guys. Let's take a break," Pete called.

We headed for the sidelines. John tossed me a towel. I always sweat like a pig when I engage in any kind of sports activity.

"So," I said to John. "Did Jayne tell you anything?" I had gone as long as I could without grilling him on the details of their conversation.

"Hey, Romeo," a voice called out before John could answer. "How's the basketball game going?"

I rolled my eyes. I was not in the mood for Garth Hunter. And I couldn't understand why he wouldn't leave me alone. My mind knew it was safer to lay low, but I was getting tired of being the butt of Garth's jokes. If I didn't stop him right now, he might go on harassing me forever.

"Why don't you come play and find out for yourself?" I called back.

Garth snorted. "You think you can take me on?"

"I *think* I don't want to have anything to do with you, Garth," I answered. "But it's a free country. You want to play, fine."

Garth's face looked like stone as he took off his jacket and tossed it onto the bleachers.

"Okay, big man," he said. "Let's see what you've got."

Garth didn't even ask if someone was willing to sit out to make room for him. He just walked onto the court and started to dribble the basketball. For the umpteenth time I was irritated by Garth's assumption that he always deserved to be the center of attention.

The rest of us joined Garth on the court. Pete took the ball, then threw it to me. I headed toward the basket. Garth was in my face every step of the way. I was just about to unload the ball when his hand darted out.

He knocked the basketball from my grip, shot it quickly to a teammate, then elbowed me out of the way. If we'd been playing regulation basketball, his move would have been a definite personal foul.

"What's the matter, big man?" Garth shouted as I trailed him back down the court. "Mind not on the game?"

"At least I have a mind," I snapped. Garth laughed.

His team scored, and I took the ball. I fired it to Brian Thompson, then got back in the game.

"Still not back with Natalie, huh?" Garth asked. He was running next to me, and his face was just inches from mine. I decided I wouldn't dignify that comment with an answer.

Pete tossed the ball to me. Garth lunged forward. Suddenly our feet were tangled together. Garth fell to the ground just as I managed to grab the ball.

"Sorry about that," I said, reaching a hand down to help him up. The fact that he had tripped was totally his own fault—but there was still such a thing as sportsmanship. Garth slapped my hand away.

"Let me clue you in about something, Smith," Garth said, getting to his feet on his own. "I can have Natalie Taylor back whenever I want her. You haven't got a chance."

"Who said I wanted one?" I said. I could feel my face start to heat up, but I wasn't about to give Garth any more ammunition than he already had.

"You are truly pathetic," Garth stated. "You're not fooling anyone. You've been following Natalie around like a dog with its tongue hanging out. It would be disgusting if it wasn't so sad."

"You're full of it," I told him. I could feel my temper rising out of control. "And Natalie would never get back with you. The whole reason she broke up with me is because she's afraid I'm going to treat her the way you did. Unfortunately we're both Geminis."

Garth's face turned red. He looked furious. "That's a total crock and you know it. That astrology thing is just an excuse. The truth is she compared the two of us. You didn't measure up, so she dumped you."

My stomach churned. Garth had just voiced my deepest fear. The fear I'd worked so hard to avoid thinking about.

"You're the one who's full of it," I shouted.

"Anytime," Garth taunted me. "I can have her back anytime I want. She wouldn't even care if she had to share me with Tanya."

"I'm through talking about this," I said, walking off the basketball court. "I came here to shoot some hoops, not to discuss your fantasy life."

"Oh, that's right," Garth called after me. "Walk away. I'm telling the truth, and you're not man enough to take it.

"Your definition of a man is a Neanderthal."

I grabbed my jacket from the bench. Without looking back, I headed for the doors. I knew I was giving Garth the upper hand by walking away from our confrontation. But I had taken all I could for one day.

I pushed open the gym's huge steel doors and stomped out of the gym. Outside, it was raining. The cold, wet afternoon matched my mood perfectly.

As I crossed the parking lot, Garth's words echoed through my head. I wanted to dismiss what he had said, but I couldn't. Garth and Natalie had been together. It was a fact. And nothing I could do would change the past.

I didn't want to believe that Natalie had broken up with me because she secretly preferred Garth Hunter. Natalie wasn't the kind of girl who would put up with Garth's obnoxious behavior for long. I told myself that Garth's ego had been talking. His claim that Natalie would get back together with him wasn't based on anything besides his own inflated opinion of himself.

But as I opened the door of my car my thoughts were a vicious circle. Even when Natalie was responding to my kisses, had she really been comparing me to Garth?

★　　★　　★

Friday night was a total washout. Seven days ago I had been looking forward to going out with Natalie. Tonight the only thing I had to look forward to was watching *The X-Files* on TV.

I sat in the living room with John, my mom, and my little brothers. This was hardly a romantic crowd. And I was still so wound up about what had happened with Garth at the basketball court that I had forgotten to fight Roy and Randy for my fair share of the popcorn.

But I wasn't the only one who seemed bummed out. John had been frowning since the second he walked in the door. All evening he had been sitting in front of the television, a glazed look in his eyes.

"Time for bed," my mom finally announced to the twins.

"We don't want to go," Roy whined.

My mom gave him one of her infamous stern glances. "No arguments," she said.

The twins obediently hopped off the couch and headed toward the stairs. They knew not to mess with Mom when she had that look in her eye.

"Hey," I said to John as soon as we were alone. "Sorry I've been kind of preoccupied tonight."

John was watching Agent Mulder chase an alien down a dark alley.

"That's okay," he said. "To tell you the truth, I hadn't really noticed."

Agent Scully appeared, waving one of those FBI issue halogen flashlights. I've always been impressed with the amount of ground she covers while running in her high heels.

"So I never did get to find out," I said. "How did things go with Jayne this afternoon?"

At the mention of Jayne, John groaned. "It was kind of hard to tell," he said. "She did say Natalie wasn't talking much about how she felt about the breakup."

Was that good or bad? I was glad Natalie wasn't going around saying that she was thrilled to death that she had dumped me. But I would have liked her to be confessing to her best friend that she was miserable without me.

"Do you think you made an impression on Jayne?" I asked.

John snorted and looked away from the television. "I made an impression, all right. I impressed her as being a total buffoon. I had the perfect opportunity to ask her out—nothing big—maybe just coffee or something. And all I could do was talk about Natalie and you."

All of a sudden I felt a little guilty. I'd been so wrapped up in my own romantic scenario, I'd failed to consider I might be using John only to further my own ends.

"Next time it will be easier," I told him, trying to cheer him up. "You've broken the ice. Established contact."

"You make her sound like an alien," John said.

"Well, face it, John; she is a girl."

Under normal circumstances John would have at least cracked a smile at my remark. But now he continued to stare at the television screen, his expression morose.

"If Garth and Natalie get back together, what happens to me and Jayne?" John asked.

So that was it. Both John and I were stewing about Garth Hunter.

"That is not going to happen, John," I said. "There is absolutely no way."

"But if they did," John insisted. "I could never ask her out. I mean, it would be like betraying my best friend."

"John," I said in a low, calm voice. "If you want to ask Jayne out, you should ask her—regardless of who Natalie's going out with. There's no rule that says you can't go out with a girl just because you hate the guts of her best friend's boyfriend."

"I'm never going to get up the nerve to ask her out," John said. "So I guess the whole issue of Natalie and Garth is irrelevant."

"Come on, John," I said. "Snap out of it. You can't give up now. You haven't done anything yet."

"You did something," John pointed out. "And look where you ended up."

I had never seen John so depressed. It was disturbing.

"You can't think like that," I insisted. "If you do, you'll never go out with anyone."

"Actually," John admitted, "that was sort of what I had in mind."

By one o'clock in the morning I was exhausted. But I couldn't sleep. I was lying in my bed, staring at my ceiling. Since John had left a few hours before, I had been thinking about his situation. Worrying about my best friend's nonexistent love life was better than worrying about my own nonexistent love life.

John was obviously not capable of asking out a girl

without a little help from a friend. At this rate he was going to wind up spending his life in a monastery.

I can't let that happen, I thought. *No matter what happens between me and Natalie, there's got to be a way to salvage any feelings that might exist between John and Jayne.*

I needed to plan an event that would bring John and Jayne together. Something special. I wanted the occasion to be the kind of thing where Jayne could see how great John was. And it would be best if John was the center of attention. But what?

Suddenly I laughed out loud.

The perfect occasion was coming up, and I would be ready for it. I was going to throw John a surprise party for his birthday.

"Have you selected the theme yet for your party?" the saleswoman asked me.

It was Saturday morning, and I was at the It's My Party supply store. I'd headed out on a mission to plan the party as soon as my mom had given me the go-ahead. There was no point in wasting time. I stared at the saleswoman's name tag. Her name was Julie—luckily Julie seemed very friendly.

Planning parties is not exactly something I've had a lot of experience with. I had a feeling I was going to need all the help I could get. March 3 wasn't all that far away. And according to Julie I had a lot to consider.

The fact that I might have to select a theme for a simple party had never once occurred to me. I had assumed I would buy a few balloons, a few paper plates, a pack of candles . . .

"Is a theme mandatory?" I asked.

Julie laughed. "Of course not. But lots of our patrons prefer to have one. A theme makes it easier to coordinate what you want to buy."

"I've never been very coordinated," I told her. She laughed again. "Is it okay if I just look around?"

"Sure. If I can be of any assistance, just let me know."

"Thanks, I will."

I walked off to investigate a window display of life-size *Star Trek, Next Generation* cardboard cutouts. Maybe Jayne would be impressed if the guest list for John's party included Data and Captain Picard.

The store felt enormous. I had no idea there were so many possible themes from which to choose. One entire row was devoted to black table-cloths, black silverware, and black cake decorations. The black napkins had a poem written on them, saying how sorry everybody was that the guest of honor was turning forty years old. And people say teenagers have incomprehensible senses of humor!

I turned the corner and tried another row. Crepe paper streamers were definitely out, I decided. I hate to sound gender biased, but streamers seemed more appropriate for a girl. But I thought balloons would be all right as long as they didn't have any cutesy sayings on them.

I came to a stop underneath a cluster of pinatas hanging from the ceiling. A pinata seemed like a good possibility. Banging a cardboard donkey would be something the party guests could do all together—sort of a party bonding experience.

Then I imagined the look on my mother's face

when she saw a bunch of teenagers waving large sticks. Not to mention what would happen after the party when Roy and Randy did their own pinata bonding.

Nope, the pinata was definitely out. I crossed the aisle and stared at a display of Donald Duck paper plates. I laughed. Donald wasn't exactly the symbol of a hip party.

The chime over the store's front door went off, signaling another customer had entered. Maybe I could follow this other person around. Scoping out the kind of choices someone else was making might give me some tips. Of course, with my luck the new customer was probably planning a seventy-fifth birthday party for his or her grandmother.

I hung a quick left, heading for a display with a Wild West theme. I didn't even see the store's second customer, who stepped into the aisle at the exact same time I did. I was going so fast, I plowed right into her.

"I'm really sorry," I said. "It's totally my fault. I wasn't watching where I was going."

The person I'd almost flattened reached out to pick up a paper palm tree that had been the other victim of the collision.

"No problem," she said. She straightened up and brushed her hair out of her face.

My heart rate accelerated. The other customer was Natalie.

She looked great as usual. Today she was wearing a chocolate-colored shirt that was the exact color of her eyes. Her soft brown hair cascaded over her shoulders. This was the closest I'd been to her since our breakup.

And if I didn't control my overloaded teenage hormones soon, I was going to do something incredibly embarrassing.

"Hi," I said. "Look, I'm really sorry."

Natalie's face lit up for a brief instant. "Honestly, it's okay, Dean."

An awkward silence fell between us. I sensed that Natalie wanted to talk but was holding herself back.

"Is everything all right over there?" Julie sang out from up at the counter.

"Fine, thank you," I called back.

Julie's voice seemed to break the weird connection that was causing Natalie and me to stare into each other's eyes. Natalie made a move to step away.

"So," I said, determined not to lose her so soon. "What brings you here?"

Natalie concentrated on a rack of hula skirts. "I'm throwing a birthday party for Jayne."

"You're kidding," I said. "But that's why I'm here."

Natalie looked up, a smile hovering around the corners of her mouth. "You're here because you're planning a party for Jayne?"

"For John," I corrected. "A surprise party—for his birthday." My mind began to race with possibilities. *This is a perfect opportunity. Don't blow it, Dean.*

"So," I said, trying to sound as casual as I could. "We could, you know, pool our resources. Don't they have the same birthday?"

"They do." Natalie sounded a bit tentative. "But I don't know, Dean."

I decided to be totally honest. "Look, Natalie, I know things are kind of awkward between us. . . . I don't want to pressure you."

100

Natalie blushed, but she met my eyes steadily. "Part of the reason I'm throwing this party is because of Jayne," I continued. "John really likes her, and I thought a party would be a good way to get the two of them together. But if we each throw a party, Jayne won't even *be* at my party. My plans will be totally ruined."

"Mine too," Natalie admitted. "I was throwing my party for the same reason as you."

There was another long silence. Natalie's expression was serious. I could almost hear her weighing the pros and cons of my proposition in her mind.

A joint party for John and Jayne would accomplish more than each of us throwing our own. It would also mean Natalie and I would have to spend a lot time together. That fact was perfect for my purposes, but I wasn't sure how Natalie felt about it.

I realized that I had better really mean it about the no-pressure part of the arrangements. At the first sign of a false move Natalie would run for cover.

"We could have it at your house," I suggested. Maybe she would feel more comfortable on her own territory. "But we would split the costs for everything—decorations, food, and whatever else we needed."

I could feel the scales begin to tip in my favor. "I guess it would be all right," Natalie said slowly. "I'd have to check with my mom."

"Of course," I said, trying to hide my elation. "I can have my mom call yours if you want."

"That would be nice," Natalie said. "I'm sure she'd appreciate that. You know, I've never met your mom."

"I guess you didn't," I answered. *We never got that far,* I thought. But I kept that observation to myself.

"So this will be really great," I said. "The perfect opportunity for Jayne and John to expand their respective social lives."

"It's kind of amazing that it turned out they really like each other, isn't it?" Natalie asked.

I nodded. "And even more amazing they can't do anything about it on their own." I paused. "So about this party. What do you think the theme should be?"

"Theme?" Natalie asked. She looked confused. "Do we need a theme?"

I grinned. "According to Julie, the It's My Party store lady, we do."

Natalie thought for a moment. "How do you suppose John feels about Pin the Tail on the Donkey?"

Nine

NATALIE

Scorpio (Oct. 23–Nov. 21)
Moon position highlights turmoil. Now is
the time to step back, do some soul searching.
One close to you suggests you try a fresh
approach. Is status quo really what you want?

"NATALIE, IF YOU break one more egg,
you're going to have to go the store for a
new dozen."

My mom's voice was patient, but I could tell she
was starting to get frustrated with me. We were in
the kitchen assembling ingredients for a mammoth
cookie-baking session for Jayne and John's birthday
party that night. Usually I'm pretty good in the
kitchen. But I'd been dropping things all morning.

I cracked the last egg in the house on the edge of
the counter. I'd learned in health class that one
should never crack an egg on the side of the bowl
because of the risk of salmonella poisoning.

I maneuvered the egg over the mixing bowl quickly. The contents slid onto the cookie dough. I went to toss the eggshells into the trash can. Unfortunately I overshot the mark, and the shells fell to the floor.

"Okay, time out," my mom said. She leaned over and scooped up the eggshells. "Stir that last egg in, then put the batter in the fridge. We're going to sit down at the table and talk about what's going on."

"It's nothing, really," I protested five minutes later.

I was sitting at the kitchen table across from my mother. Even as I said the words, I knew she wasn't going to let me get away with denying that anything was wrong. My mom has a way of making me spill my guts. I'm never sure how she does it, but before I know what's happening, I'm telling her everything.

"I'm just nervous about this party, that's all," I continued.

"Um-hm," my mom said. She sounded totally unconvinced. She got up, walked to the fridge, and pulled out two sodas. She set one down in front of me, returned to her seat, and popped the top of hers.

"I thought the party was your idea," she said when she was settled. "Why should you be nervous about it?"

"A party just for Jayne was my idea," I countered. "A joint party was Dean's idea."

"Ah, Dean," Mom said. She took a sip of her soda.

Uh-oh, I thought. *Here it comes.*

"He's coming over to help you bake these cookies, isn't he?" she asked.

The thought of Dean and I baking cookies together had been messing with my equilibrium all afternoon. It seemed like such an old married couple thing to do. The sort of thing a girl would do with her longtime steady boyfriend—not with the guy she'd had to break up with.

"Yeah, he'll be here in about half an hour," I answered, still not certain how much I wanted to confide in my mother. "So I don't think we really have time for extensive therapy, Mom."

My mother looked at me, her head tilted over to one side. It was her evaluating-the-situation look. "So," she said. "The fact that you've been dropping things all afternoon doesn't have anything to do with your relationship with Dean?"

"We don't have a relationship," I said, popping the top on my own soda. "We broke up, if you recall."

"That doesn't necessarily mean you don't still have a relationship," my mother insisted. "Natalie, I'm not going to make an issue out of this if you really don't want to tell me what's going on."

She paused. I could tell she was about to say something insightful and motherly. "I would just like to say that it's not like you to be afraid to face up to something."

What is it about mothers? After a woman gives birth, she automatically activates some guilt-trip gene. Mom was right, of course. I wasn't really facing up to how I was feeling—particularly how I was feeling about Dean.

We had gotten together a couple of times in the past few days to work out the details of the party. Dean had been really easy to be with every time.

He didn't do anything to make me feel bad about the fact that we'd broken up. And he never put any pressure on me to get back together with him.

His behavior should have been exactly what I wanted. Instead, Dean's overly polite demeanor only made me cranky and depressed. Dean could never have felt as strongly about me as I did about him. If he had, he wouldn't have given up this easily.

I couldn't talk the situation over with Jayne because then I'd have to reveal the reason that Dean and I had been together. The only other person I could really confide in was my mom. Maybe that's how she gets me to tell her everything. Being a mother gives her excellent leverage for being in the right place at the right time.

"I guess I *am* a little confused about what's happening with Dean and me," I said at last. "I thought he really liked me, but lately it hasn't seemed that way at all."

"Wait a minute," my mom said. "Weren't you the one who wanted to break up?"

"Well, yes," I answered. "But it was never because I didn't like him, Mom. I broke it off because Dean's a Gemini. He and I are a bad astrological combination. I learned that the hard way . . . with Garth."

My mother was silent for a moment. I took a sip of my soda, gasping a little as the carbonation burned my throat on the way down.

"Natalie, you know I've never interfered in your interest in astrology," my mother started. "But I have to say that your obsession with the stars has concerned me from time to time. You take everything so literally, honey."

106

I gazed down at the table. My mom sounded like she was actually worried about me.

"Doesn't it seem to you that astrology works best when you just use it as a general guide?" she asked.

I thought about her question while I downed a second swallow of soda. I'd been having similar thoughts myself. I just didn't understand how being with Dean could feel so right when he was the wrong sign. It almost seemed possible that signs didn't mean much after all. But if I backed down from my position now, I would look like a total idiot.

"Use it as a guide?" I asked. "I'm not sure what you mean. Either you believe in something or you don't. Isn't that right?"

"I'm not saying you have to stop believing in it," my mother said. "But in my experience, nothing in life really functions the way you describe the significance of astrological signs. The world isn't black and white."

I nodded. She was making a lot of sense. She usually does.

"Did Dean ever do anything to make you think that he would treat you the way Garth did?" she asked.

"No," I admitted. "I was just so sure he would be a jerk, sooner or later, because he's a Gemini."

"So if Dean wasn't a Gemini, the two of you would still be together?" she asked.

"Maybe," I answered.

"Try yes or no," my mom insisted.

I squirmed in my chair like a kindergartner who had just been caught stealing her best friend's graham crackers at snack time.

"Okay, well, probably yes. But Dean hasn't seemed very upset about the fact that we're not together." I took a deep breath. "We've been planning this party for weeks, and he hasn't mentioned our breakup once."

My mother shook her head. "It seems to me you're trying to have things both ways, Natalie," she said. "You want to be free to break up with Dean, but you want to keep him tied to you. You want him to be upset over your breakup, even though you have no intention of getting back together with him."

It was quite a speech. There was just one problem with everything my mom had said. She was absolutely right.

"So what am I supposed to do?" I asked.

"I don't know that there's anything you can do—unless you're willing to rethink this whole astrology thing," she said. "Personally, I think you should be more willing to trust your own instincts. You're never going to learn how to be in any relationship if you always base it on astrology and not on what you're really feeling."

At that instant the doorbell rang. "Oh, my gosh," I said. "It's five o'clock already. That's Dean."

"I'll make myself scarce," my mother promised. She got up and gave my shoulders a quick squeeze. "Trust your heart, honey. It's usually in the right place, even when the stars aren't."

"Ha ha," I said. "Very funny."

"Those cookies are supposed to be for the party, you know," I observed a few hours later. Dean and

I were in the kitchen, surrounded by sheets of cookies. First we had made peanut butter cookies. Then we moved on to oatmeal raisin. We'd finished with several dozen chocolate chip.

Dean and I had assembled quite an awesome amount of good stuff to eat. But every time I walked by the trays of cooling chocolate chip cookies, another one seemed to be missing.

"I haven't taken any," Dean insisted. "I don't know what you're talking about."

It was hard not to laugh every time I looked at him. Hoping that my hormones might stay under control if Dean didn't look as good as he usually did, I'd made him wear my mother's frilliest apron. So far the apron seemed to have been a good call. I had been able to concentrate on getting the cookies baked without being too distracted by my desire to kiss Dean.

But I was still extremely confused. My feelings for Dean—both good and bad—were near the surface of my every thought. I could sense them in the background, sort of like static on the radio.

I turned on the faucet and rinsed out a mixing bowl. Maybe my mother was right. Maybe I should use astrology just as a general guide. I could assume that *in general,* Geminis were a bad match for me— but I might be able to make a romance work with one particular, very exceptional Gemini.

Dean turned from the table where the cookies were cooling. He was a vision of ruffly blue-and-white-checked gingham. My mother always referred to the apron Dean was wearing as her Suzy Homemaker special. A dab of chocolate clung to one corner of Dean's mouth.

I forced myself to quit daydreaming and focus on the conversation Dean and I were having. "You haven't eaten any cookies?" I asked. "Then how come you've got chocolate on your face?"

"I don't," Dean protested, trying to wipe away the evidence. "Where do I have chocolate on my face?"

I grabbed a paper towel and ran it under the faucet. Then I walked over to Dean. "Right about here." I reached up to his face with the paper towel.

"Wait a minute," Dean said. He laughed and held up his arm to block my hand. I tried unsuccessfully to get my hand past the wall of his arm.

After several moments of struggling over possession of the paper towel, Dean pushed me gently against the sink. He pinned my arms behind my back.

"If you think I'm going to let you attack me with that soggy towel for no good reason, forget it," he said. "Just show me where the chocolate is."

He allowed me to pull one hand (the one not holding the paper towel) from behind my back. I placed my fingertips at the corner of his mouth. "Right there, Dean," I said softly.

The instant I touched him, I knew I had made a mistake. Dean's eyes practically burned a hole through me. The friendly, easygoing guy he had been for the last few days completely vanished.

Dean's lips moved slowly toward mine. I knew I should back away, but I was paralyzed. A moment later we were kissing.

Dean's kiss was warm and possessive—the kind of kiss that staked a claim. His kiss told me in no uncertain terms how he felt about our breakup. I knew that as far as he was concerned, the horrible scene in the cafeteria had never happened. He was still in love with me.

I knew I shouldn't kiss him back—not until I had decided what I really wanted. But I couldn't seem to help myself. My mom had recommended I listen to my instincts . . . and right this minute my instincts were shouting that I wanted to kiss Dean.

Dean's arms were around me. He was no longer pinning me to the sink; instead he was pressing me against his body. I wound my free hand around Dean's neck.

His skin was warm, and his hair was smooth and silky. Holding Dean felt so good, so right. I found myself wishing we could stay this way forever. I didn't want this kiss to end.

Finally Dean pulled away. I was breathless, and my heart was pounding in my chest. Dean hugged me close. I pressed my face against his neck. Dean pulled the scrunchie from my ponytail, then ran his fingers through my hair as it spilled down across my shoulders.

"I've waited weeks to do that," he said.

"What?" I somehow managed to say. "To kiss me or to mess up my hair?"

"Both."

Dean kissed me again. This time his lips were gentle, but no less certain. I knew in my heart that I belonged with Dean. He belonged with me. We belonged together. So much for astrology.

"Natalie, we can't ignore what's happening," Dean said when the kiss was over. "We've got to talk about this."

"I know," I said. "I know we do, Dean. It's just—" I felt the muscles in Dean's body tense as

111

he sensed my reluctance to have a "talk."

"Could we wait until after the party?" I continued. "If it looks like we're back together, all the attention will be focused on us. Tonight is supposed to be for John and Jayne."

"I suppose you have a point," Dean said, his voice low. "But I'd like to go on record as saying that I don't like it very much."

The timer on the stove buzzed, signaling the successful completion of the last sheetful of chocolate chip cookies. Dean backed up and released me.

"I'll get those," he said. He took the cookie sheet out of the oven and set it on the stovetop.

We waited a few moments for the cookies to cool. Then I lifted them off the sheet with a spatula.

"You look great in the kitchen," Dean commented. "You're a younger version of June Cleaver."

"And you're Julia Child," I said.

We both laughed as I removed the last cookie. I switched off the stove, then untied the string of Dean's apron.

As soon as he was free from the frilly blue gingham Dean pulled me into his arms again. He kissed me slowly—a kiss of promise. He might have agreed that we could put off discussing the details of our relationship for the moment, but there was definitely no going back from here.

"So I guess I'll see you later, huh?" he said.

"Um," I murmured. "Unless you're planning to diss our party."

"I would never diss our party," he replied. "I was a Boy Scout." He gave me another quick kiss on the cheek. "Do you want me to come back in a little while and help you set up?"

"My mom will help," I answered, trying to get the situation back on a more businesslike footing. "Your most important assignment is the successful delivery of John."

"He'll be here," Dean promised, releasing me from his arms. "Even if I have to tie him up and stuff him in a box."

"Just make sure you wrap him nicely," I said. We walked toward the front door. "And put a big bow on top."

"Too bad we didn't think of this earlier," Dean said as I pulled open the front door. "We could have had him pop out of a cake."

"Not a chance," I told him. "Think what would happen if he got frosting in that hair."

"What's wrong with his hair?" Dean asked, his eyes teasing.

I gave him a push. "Good-bye, Dean," I said.

"Au revoir, Natalie," Dean answered as he walked down the front walk.

"I didn't know you were bilingual," I called after him.

It wasn't until I had shut the door that I realized Dean hadn't actually said good-bye. Instead he had said, "Until we meet again."

I smiled to myself. If I had things my way, Dean and I would certainly be meeting again. And again. And again . . .

"Cologne is always nice," the saleslady at the department store suggested.

"No," I said. "I don't think he's a male fragrance kind of guy."

I had made a last-minute dash to the mall. The preparations for the party were in good shape. And I was too keyed up from what had happened between Dean and me just to sit around and do nothing at home.

I would still have plenty of time to shower and make myself completely gorgeous. So I had decided to use the extra time to find a gift for Dean.

I had always planned to give him something to say thank you for cohosting the party. But now I was looking for something special—something that would reflect the fact that we were back together again.

I was still pretty nervous about the whole situation. There were lots of details to be worked out. But that first kiss in the kitchen had settled something between Dean and me. I would be an idiot to pretend it hadn't.

For better or for worse, I was going to start seeing Dean again.

Unfortunately I was having no luck finding a present for him. Everything I came across seemed too generic, too bland, or too corny. I couldn't just give him a book or some men's cologne. I needed something quirky. Something that just said "Dean."

"Thanks a lot," I said to the lady behind the men's fragrance counter. "I guess I'll just have to keep looking." I headed back out into the mall to scope out some of the smaller shops. If all else failed, maybe I could get Dean something sort of goofy and romantic, like a repeat of the boutonniere I'd gotten him for the Sweethearts' Dance.

The boutonniere could symbolize the fact that we were starting over.

I decided a cup of coffee was in order. I needed to mull over my latest idea. I was heading toward the nearest espresso stand for some caffeine-related inspiration when a hand descended on my shoulder.

"Hey, where are you off to in such a hurry?" The voice behind me was low and masculine.

My stomach dropped to my feet. I turned around and found myself face-to-face with Garth Hunter.

Garth looked the way he always did—like a male model. His face was so perfect and his outfit so carefully put together that he almost didn't seem real. I couldn't picture Garth spending hours in my kitchen, baking cookies in my mother's apron. And I absolutely couldn't imagine wanting to kiss him when we were done.

I resisted the temptation to tell Garth to get his slimy paw off my shoulder. Instead I simply stepped back. Garth's hand dropped back down to his side.

"Hello, Garth," I said coldly. "Did you want something?"

"Hey," Garth said again. "That's no way to greet an old love. I'm just being friendly, Natalie." He grinned. "How are you? I haven't seen you in a while."

"You see me in school five days a week," I pointed out. "And I'm fine." I gave him a grim smile. "Was there anything else?"

Garth's eyes focused at some point beyond my head for a split second. Then his gaze zeroed in on my face.

"As a matter of fact, there is something else," he said. He ran one hand up and down my arm in an irritatingly intimate gesture.

I stepped back again, hoping Garth would get the hint. Instead he moved even closer. "The truth is, I've kind of missed you, Natalie."

I began to wonder if I was having a hallucination. Maybe the mall had some sort of high-powered ultrasonic security system that was messing up my brain waves.

"You've missed me?" I asked, my voice full of disbelief. "You've got to be kidding."

"Oh, come on," Garth said, his voice warm and coaxing. "Don't be like that, Natalie. I never really wanted us to break up, you know. I only ended our relationship because of Tanya."

"That was pretty obvious," I said dryly.

"But Tanya's going out of town for spring break," Garth continued. "She'll be gone for a whole week. I thought maybe you and I could use that time to reevaluate our relationship. . . . You've always understood me so well."

You bet I do, I thought. *I understand you perfectly.*

I gave Garth a great big smile. He smiled back, as if he were triumphant. On impulse I stepped forward and wrapped my arms around his neck.

"I tell you what," I whispered in his ear. "I've got an even better idea. While Tanya's gone on spring break, you can take your brilliant idea down a long walk on a short pier." I pulled back and gave him another smile. "Drop dead, Garth."

Ten

DEAN

Gemini (May 21–June 20)
Disaster looms large on the horizon—just when
it seemed that everything was going your way.
Don't jump to automatic conclusions. Give
loved ones the benefit of the doubt. Look for
escape clause.

I FELT AS if I had been kicked in the stomach. I
was standing outside Fleur du Jour at the mall,
having spent a small fortune on a dozen long-
stemmed red roses. The first thing I had seen when
I walked out of the door of the florist's shop was
Natalie throwing herself into Garth Hunter's arms.

The smell of the roses seemed to rise up and
smother me. I was gripping the flowers so tightly
that I could feel the thorns even through the wrap-
ping paper.

Less than two hours ago Natalie and I had been
standing in her kitchen. She'd had her arms

wrapped around me. I would have sworn she had been putting her whole heart into our kisses. But before my very eyes was evidence of who Natalie's heart really belonged to.

It belonged to Garth Hunter. Not to me.

I turned around and walked in the opposite direction of Garth and Natalie. Maybe I'd give the roses to my mother. Or take them to the party and say they were a gift from John to Jayne.

Just the thought of going to the party at Natalie's made me physically ill. But I knew I had to go through with the farce. I owed it to John.

When I reached the mall exit, I hit the double glass doors with a force that made my arm ache. I walked out into the parking lot and headed for my car.

I tried to imagine how I would feel when I saw Natalie again. She would probably smile at me, never guessing that I knew what was going on.

I shook my head sadly. Never in my wildest dreams would I have thought that Natalie could be so two-faced.

I had been totally wrong about the kind of girl she was. I'd been wrong about her all along.

I tossed the roses into a nearby garbage can and unlocked the front door of the car. Then I started the engine and peeled out of the parking lot.

As I drove through the streets of Seattle, I realized that I had stopped dreading going to the party tonight. Now I was actually looking forward to it. I wanted to see the look on Natalie's face when I told her I had witnessed her and Garth Hunter's love fest.

After I gave her that news, I'd drop another bombshell. I would tell her I never wanted to see her again.

"I can't believe you did this," John exclaimed several hours later.

We were hanging out in one corner of Natalie's living room, drinking sodas. Jayne was standing over by the stereo, putting on a new CD. She was wearing a blue dress that matched her eyes, and her cheeks had a rosy glow. She kept looking over at John and giving him shy smiles.

So far the party was a success. Except for Natalie and me, everyone was having a great time. John and Jayne had hardly been apart all evening.

And I had to admit that it had been a brilliant idea of Natalie's to have the guests play little kid party games. We had divided into teams, girls against the guys. John had led the boys and Jayne had led the girls. The girls had been better at Pin the Tail on the Donkey, but the guys had been victorious at the apple-bobbing contest.

"So," I said as a cut from the newest Cranberries album blasted out from the stereo. "How are things between you and Jayne?"

"Definitely looking good," John said. He grinned as Jayne began to move toward us. "I suppose you're going to tell me you set up this whole thing."

"Well, I did have help," I admitted.

"Oh, yeah," John said. He glanced over at the dining-room table, where Natalie was replenishing an empty bowl of potato chips. "Things, uh, seem a little tense between you and Natalie."

To say that things were tense between Natalie and me was the understatement of the year.

When the big moment had arrived, I hadn't

119

actually charged into Natalie's house and accused her of cheating on me. I had reminded myself that this was John's big night. I knew I should wait to see how things in his love life were progressing before I turned my attention to my own.

It had been a difficult decision to make, given the way that I was feeling. But I had figured that I owed it to John. He was my best friend. He had never lied to me. If I told Natalie off at John's expense, I was making her more important than he was.

I had settled for avoiding her all evening instead. But the moment I had come inside, Natalie had slipped her arm around my back and given me a quick hug. I hadn't been able to stop her. I hadn't hugged her back.

She had been shooting me puzzled glances all night. The thing that upset me the most was that the hurt expression on her face was actually starting to get to me.

Natalie looked so innocent, so confused. Her big brown eyes were full of questions. But I kept telling myself not to let down my guard. Everything she was doing now was just an act.

I wondered when she planned to tell me that she and Garth were back together. Maybe the plan was not to tell me at all. She would keep stringing me along.

Then she and Garth would laugh together about what a fool I was. Just thinking about the two of them together made my stomach turn.

Natalie finished filling the bowl of chips and disappeared into the kitchen. She came back a moment later carrying a plate of cookies. The sight of the cookies we had baked together kicked the burning in my stomach up a notch.

Don't do this to yourself, Dean, I thought. *She's not worth it.*

I forced myself to smile at Jayne as she came over to where John and I were standing. I could feel John go on full alert, like someone had plugged him into a power outlet.

"Happy birthday," I said. "You look really great, Jayne."

"Thanks, Dean," Jayne said, her voice pleased but quiet. "And thanks for giving me the CD."

"You're welcome," I said. "Pretty good dance music, huh?"

Jayne blushed. "I like it," she said.

John looked as if his shirt collar was too tight. "Do you, maybe, want to dance?" he asked Jayne.

Jayne looked straight at him, her blue eyes shining. "I would love to dance."

John grinned. In what was for him a totally bold move, he captured Jayne's hand. They headed toward the den Natalie had converted into a dance floor. I was left standing alone in the corner, staring across the room at Natalie.

I swallowed a mouthful of soda and pondered the situation. *Now's the time to do it,* I said to myself. *John and Jayne are obviously in great shape. They don't need any more help from you.*

I started to walk forward, but Natalie moved first. We met in the center of the living room.

Natalie's beautiful dark brown eyes looked worried. There were tiny lines of tension etched around her mouth. "Dean, is something wrong?" she asked. "You've been avoiding me all night."

"I'm surprised you noticed I was here at all," I said. My voice sounded ugly, but I couldn't help it. "Aren't you waiting for somebody more important?"

Natalie's frown deepened. "I don't know what you're talking about," she said.

Part of me actually admired her. Even face-to-face with my anger, she wasn't going to reveal anything. She was going to play Miss Innocent.

"Think about it, Natalie," I said. "Isn't there anything you'd like to tell me? Something I might consider important that has to do with our relationship?"

"Our relationship?" Natalie said.

"Oh, that's right, I forgot," I said sarcastically. "We don't really have one, do we? It's just something I made up."

"Dean," Natalie said, her voice full of frustration. "I don't understand why you're so angry. You've got to tell me what this is all about."

At that moment the front door opened. We both turned our heads to see who had arrived.

"Hey, is there a party here or what?" a voice called out.

I saw Natalie's eyes widen. Then her face went blank. "Oh, no," she said.

The voice belonged to Garth Hunter.

Eleven

NATALIE

Scorpio (Oct. 23–Nov. 21)
Chaos! You discover you've been living in a
fool's paradise. Your dream castle is nothing
but a house of cards. But beneath your feet
a sturdy foundation may still exist. Face
your troubles head-on.

*T*HIS IS A *nightmare,* I thought as I stared at
Garth. *This isn't happening. It can't be real.*

I was standing in the middle of my living room,
fighting about I still didn't know *what* with Dean.

And I knew in my gut that whatever Dean was
upset about would not be helped by the presence of
Garth.

Why did Garth have to pick tonight to crash a
party? I had the feeling Garth would do anything to
interfere with me and Dean.

"Excuse me a minute," I said, moving past
Dean. "There's something I have to take care of."

"Take your time," Dean said. It was another one of those cryptic remarks he'd been making all evening. Everything out of his mouth had sounded angry and bitter.

"This is a private party, Garth," I said, taking his arm and trying to ease him toward the front door. I didn't want to make a scene. Other people had seen him come in, and I didn't want him to ruin Jayne's party. And I definitely didn't want Garth anywhere near Dean.

This is going to be a first, I thought. *Garth has probably never been kicked out of a party before.*

"I'm sorry," I said as I propelled him as far away from Dean as I could. "But I can only have a certain number of people over. I promised my mom and dad."

"What a good little girl you are, Natalie." Garth's breath smelled sour, like stale beer.

What did I ever see in you? I thought. Beneath his glossy surface Garth was nothing but a spoiled brat.

"So what this means, Garth," I continued, "is that you'll have to party somewhere else."

Garth laughed and turned around quickly, pulling his arm out of my grasp. In surprise I stopped and stepped back, bumping up against the hall wall.

Garth put his arms on either side of my head, leaning his body toward mine. I was caged in.

"So tell me something, good-girl Natalie," Garth said, his mouth just inches from my face. "How are things going tonight with Dandy Dean?"

"What's it to you?" I asked. "Back up. Your beer breath is making me nauseous."

Garth laughed and moved a little closer. "He saw us this evening, you know."

I literally felt my blood run cold. I felt like I was in the middle of a horror novel. Now Dean's strange behavior made perfect sense.

If Dean had seen Garth and me at the mall this evening, he would have every reason to think that Garth and I were back together. He would have thought I'd betrayed him by running straight from his kisses into Garth's arms.

"You unbelievable jerk," I said. "I want you out of my house."

"Hey, I'm going," Garth said. "I just wanted to say good-bye."

Before I could stop him, he leaned down and kissed me. Then he broke contact and walked out the front door. I think I actually heard him laugh as he pulled the door closed behind him. But I was almost too upset to notice.

I had to find Dean and explain the situation. I had to make him believe that there was nothing wrong. I started back toward the living room. I took two steps, then stopped short.

Dean was standing at the end of the hall. He had seen Garth kiss me.

"Dean," I croaked. My voice was tight and filled with panic. Dean brushed past me, heading for the front door. "It's not what you think," I cried. "Let me tell you what happened."

"Save it," Dean said as he yanked open the front door. "I know exactly what happened, Natalie. You've been jerking me around."

"That's not true," I said. I followed him out onto the porch. I pulled the door closed behind me

125

so that no one at the party could overhear our fight.

It was cold outside. The exhaust from Garth's car still hung in the air above the driveway. Dean started toward his car, which was parked at the curb.

"Dean, you can't just leave like this," I said, running after him. "You've got to give me a chance to explain."

"Explain what?" he shouted. He spun around to face me. Beneath the streetlight his face looked pale. "The fact that you kissed me this afternoon and then went running off to find Garth Hunter? I'd say that situation speaks for itself, Natalie. You guys have been together all along, haven't you? All you've been doing is making a fool out of me."

When he finished his monologue, I took a deep breath. "No, Dean," I said, as calmly as I could. Maybe if I avoided getting angry, I could make him see reason. "Garth and I are not together. I did not go running off to find him. I ran into Garth by accident at the mall."

"And you accidentally threw yourself at him?" Dean answered. "What did you do, trip and fall into his arms? How many other times have you 'tripped' lately that you'd care to mention? Or weren't you going to say anything at all?"

"There's nothing to say, Dean," I said, still trying to hold it together. "I know it looks bad, but it's not what you think. If you'll just calm down a minute and let me explain—"

"Forget it, Natalie," Dean interrupted. "I'm not interested."

My hot Scorpio temper finally surged to the surface. Nobody had ever talked this way to me before. I'd had fights, sure. But nobody had ever told me they weren't interested.

"Okay, fine, don't listen to me," I yelled. "Don't be interested in the truth. See if I care."

"You *don't* care," Dean said. "That's obviously the problem. But I can solve it for you. I'm outta here."

I couldn't believe he was actually going to walk out in the middle of our argument. He was behaving exactly the way I'd always been afraid he would: like an unreasonable, two-faced Gemini.

"I can't believe you're doing this," I said, trailing him to the curbside.

Dean walked out into the street to the driver's side of his mother's car. "I can't believe you're just going to give up on us without even giving me the benefit of the doubt."

"Benefit of the doubt?" Dean almost shouted across the top of the car. "That's pretty funny, coming from you. When did you ever give *me* the benefit of the doubt? You're the one who broke up with me because I was the wrong astrological sign."

"And I see now that I was absolutely right."

"Okay," Dean said, abandoning his efforts to get the driver's-side door open. He stormed around to the back of the car. "Let's put this little theory to the test. Who's your perfect astrological guy?"

"He's a Taurus," I answered without a moment's hesitation. "April 20 to May 20. He should be born on May 5 at nine o'clock."

"A.M. or P.M.?" Dean asked.

"Nine o'clock A.M.," I told him clearly. "Pacific daylight time."

Dean folded his arms across his chest. "Well,

gee," he said sarcastically. "A guy like that shouldn't be too hard to find. If I can locate him for you, will you go out with him?"

"You have got to be kidding," I said. "Go out with my perfect astral dream date? I'd be crazy not to."

Dean nodded. "Okay, so we're on. I'll find this guy and deliver him to you. If you want, I'll even tie him up with a bow."

"I don't think a bow will be necessary, thank you," I said.

Dean waved his arm. "Whatever. I'll help Mr. Right arrange the most romantic evening you can imagine. You can specify all the details. But if the two of you go out and your evening is anything less than absolutely perfect, then you agree to give us another chance."

"Wait a minute," I said, not sure I was hearing him right. "I thought you didn't want another chance. I thought you were so sure I was still in love with Garth Hunter."

"Yes or no, Natalie?" Dean said.

"Yes," I answered. It was a ridiculous proposition. But there was no way that I could lose. Nobody, not even Dean, stood a chance against my perfect astrological match. *If* he could be found.

This would also be the perfect opportunity to prove that I'd been right to put my faith in astrology. I would get my perfect date and positive astrological reinforcement for my past decisions all at the same time.

"Shake on it," Dean said. Standing in the street behind his mother's car, we shook hands.

My mind flashed to the first time we had shaken

hands—when we'd been planning Jayne and John's first big meeting at the Sweethearts' Dance. A lot had happened since that night.

Dean walked back to the driver's side and managed to unlock the car door. "Just one more thing," he said. "How am I going to know what really happens on this dream date of yours?"

I smiled, actually feeling good for the first time since we began this ridiculous altercation. "We already shook on it, Dean. You can't add any new terms. But I think I have a solution."

"What?" Dean asked, sounding slightly suspicious.

"You'll have to trust me to tell you the truth."

Twelve

DEAN

Gemini (May 21–June 20)
Romantic situation darkens. You may be dreaming
the impossible dream. A plan to lift you out of
doldrums could backfire. Remember what happens to
the best-laid plans of mice and men.

"YOU'RE SURE THIS is going to work?" I
asked as John and I crept down the hallway
toward the school attendance office.

"Absolutely," John promised. "There's no way
we can fail."

We were taking advantage of a scheduled fire
drill to accomplish the first part of my bet with
Natalie. We were going to search the school records
to come up with a list of guys who qualified to be
her perfect astrological date.

Using the school's computers had been John's
idea, but it had taken us several days to figure out a
way to access their data. Hacking in from home

seemed too risky. I wanted to get even with Natalie, sure. But I preferred a plan that didn't involve me going to jail. When a fire drill had been announced over the P.A. system Wednesday morning, it had seemed like the perfect break.

John and I had huddled in the cafeteria at lunch, drawing maps on napkins and working out our strategy. The whole adventure had made me feel like a member of the Mission Impossible team.

The fire drill was scheduled for two o'clock. The plan was to use the five-minute break between the first and second periods after lunch to hide out in the first-floor guys' bathroom. When the fire alarm went off, John and I would hide in the stalls.

While everybody else was outside, waiting for the bell to signal the all clear, John and I would sneak into the attendance office. Then John would get into the computer database.

John planned to go through the records and pull the names of all juniors and seniors born on May 5. I had resisted the impulse to extend the search to underclassmen. There was no sense in antagonizing Natalie any further by trying to show her that a freshman was her only possible dream date.

So far the plan was going well. The fire alarm was still screeching. John was into the database. Still, I was sweating just a little. I kept having visions of encountering some school official who had decided the fire drill was a perfect opportunity to stay at their desk and enjoy a quick coffee break.

"Okay," John said as his fingers moved rapidly over the keyboard. "You want male juniors and seniors born on May 5, right?"

I nodded. "Right," I said. John typed a little more, then hit the enter button. The screen went blank. Just the cursor pulsed in the corner. "You broke it. What did you do?" I said.

"Jeez, Dean," John muttered. "Will you relax? It's just searching. This will only take a few minutes."

"Oh, only a few minutes. Is that all?" I said.

The fire alarm suddenly stopped screeching. There was dead silence in the halls. In another few minutes the all clear would sound and people would start coming back into the building.

By the time that happened, we had to be back in the bathroom so we could come out again and mingle with the other students as if we had been part of the drill all along.

"Come on, come on," I murmured, my eyes glued to the computer screen. A column of names appeared without warning on the left-hand side.

"Gotcha," John said. "You want a hard copy, don't you?"

"Yeah," I replied. John gave the command to print. The list shot out of the laser printer just as another bell went off.

I snagged the list and headed for the doorway of the attendance office. John hit the escape key and followed close behind. We sprinted down the hallway toward the bathroom. As the door closed behind us the voices of the first students back into the building resounded through the halls.

"Man," John said, wiping sweat off his forehead. "I cannot believe we pulled that off."

"Not bad for a couple of amateurs, huh?" I said.

John laughed. "You got that right. But you'd

have to have nerves of steel to do that kind of stuff on a regular basis."

"Okay," I said. "So we probably don't have future careers in the CIA. Ready to put the last phase into operation?"

John nodded. We pulled open the bathroom door and stepped out into the hall. We let the tide of students carry us back to our classroom. Then we settled into our seats as if we'd been with the rest of the class all along.

I was feeling good until I remembered the true reason for Dean and John's excellent adventure. Somewhere on the list currently residing in the back pocket of my jeans was the name of Natalie's dream date.

The guy she was betting she would fall in love with instead of me.

"You are totally insane, Dean," John said several hours later. "You aren't seriously considering setting Natalie up with Tony LaScaglia."

I didn't like the situation any better than John did. Unlike him, however, I knew there wasn't any way out of it. "I don't know for sure that it's going to end up being Tony," I answered. "But I have to talk to him. There's only three guys on the list. And he's one of them."

I had spent every spare moment during the afternoon interviewing potential date candidates by pretending I was taking a survey for my sociology class.

So far, the closest I'd come to finding Natalie's perfect match was Mark Crawford. He'd been born on May 5 at seven A.M.

Now that I had interviewed all the candidates but one, I was feeling pretty stupid. This whole thing was a terrible idea. What guy in his right mind deliberately went out and tried to find someone to replace him? Only idiots who lost their tempers. I could see now it was a good thing I didn't get angry very often.

Tony LaScaglia was the last name on the list. I'd saved him until the end on purpose—even though doing that made me feel like a wimp.

Tony LaScaglia was definite dream date material. It didn't take a rocket scientist to figure that out. If I'd had to choose a worst-nightmare scenario for who Natalie's perfect astrological mate would turn out to be, Tony LaScaglia was the guy I would have picked.

He was perfect. There were just no two ways about it. He was the first-string quarterback and captain of the baseball team. And he was a senior. That fact alone was bound to give him a slight edge. In my experience, girls were always attracted to older men.

But the worst thing about Tony LaScaglia was that everybody liked him. Even *I* liked him. And now I had to go up to him and kind of casually ask what time he had been born. If he was anywhere in the vicinity of nine A.M. Pacific daylight time, I figured I was going to have to slit my wrists.

"Don't ask him," John said as we walked outside. The weather was actually halfway decent, and lots of students were taking advantage of that fact to sit outside. Tony was helping to assemble one of the booths for the spring carnival, which was only a week and a half away.

"You and I are the only ones who've seen the

list," John reminded me. "Natalie never needs to know about Tony LaScaglia."

I shook my head, wishing it were that simple. "I can't do that, John. My pact with Natalie is based on trust. If she found out later that I'd deliberately left off a guy like Tony, she'd never speak to me again."

"She'll probably never speak to you again anyway," John predicted. "Not if she goes out with Tony LaScaglia."

"You're making me feel so much better," I said. "Thanks for the great big vote of confidence, John."

Tony LaScaglia had his shirt sleeves rolled up. His musculed forearms were drawing quite a crowd. I cast a quick look around to see if Natalie was anywhere in the vicinity. I couldn't spot her. She and Jayne must have still been inside.

"Hey, Tony," I said, walking over to where he was working. The booth he was setting up was painted blue with gold stars. It reminded me of Madame Sonya's House of Fortune.

At the sound of my greeting, Tony stopped swinging his hammer and smiled. His teeth were so white, the sun glare off them was blinding.

"What's going on?" Tony asked pleasantly.

"I'm taking a survey for Mr. Johnson's sociology class," I answered. "On personality types. What time were you born?"

"What time was I born?" Tony echoed, laughing. The girls around him giggled. "What's that supposed to prove?"

"Some scientist has this theory that people born in the morning have more competitive personalities," I lied.

Tony tossed the hammer from one hand to the other. "Really?" he said. "Wow. Well, I guess there must be something to that. I was born about nine."

"East Coast or West Coast time?" I asked him, trying to ignore the way my stomach was descending to my shoes.

"West Coast," Tony answered. "I was born right here in Seattle, in fact."

"Congratulations," I said, my stomach hitting blacktop. It was my worst-case scenario come to life. Tony LaScaglia was Natalie's perfect astrological date. "You've just moved on to the next stage of the survey."

"Great," said Tony. "What do I get?"

I sighed. "Step over here and I'll explain it to you."

"Now let me get this straight," Tony said five minutes later. The two of us were standing at the far edge of the courtyard outside Emerald High. Tony had relinquished the hammering to John.

"You like Natalie Taylor, but you want me to go out with her?" he asked.

"Natalie really has this thing about astrology," I repeated. "I already explained."

"Well, yeah," Tony said. "But that doesn't mean I understand any of it."

I groaned silently. This was harder than I had thought it would be.

"Look, Tony," I said. "Here's what happened— Natalie and I got together. Then she broke up with me when she found out I wasn't the right sign. I'm trying to prove that it doesn't make any difference what sign somebody is, so I offered to set her up with her perfect astrological guy. That guy turned out to be you."

"Me," Tony said.

"That's right," I answered.

"Wow."

"So what do you say? Will you take her out?"

"Well, sure," Tony answered. "But I still don't get what's in it for you. What if we go out and have a great time?"

"Then I agree to stay away from Natalie," I said. "But if your time is anything less than totally fantastic, I'm still in the picture."

"Oh, I get it," Tony said with his high-powered smile. "You're hoping I'll take her out and she'll be bored."

"No, I'm not hoping that," I countered. Tony raised his eyebrows in disbelief. "Well, okay," I admitted. "Just a little, maybe I am. But you've got to give this your best shot, Tony. You can't blow this off. Natalie will be able to tell."

Tony shook his head. "Dean, I really like you, man, so I've got to say this. I think that you are totally out of your mind."

"I know it must seem that way," I said. "But I know what I'm doing. So what do you say? Are we on?"

"Sure," Tony said. "I've got nothing to lose. I'm a little short of cash at the moment, though. Who's paying for this big romantic date?"

"I guess I am."

As Tony and I discussed details of his evening with Natalie, I could only hope I didn't end up paying in more ways than one.

Thirteen

NATALIE

Scorpio (Oct. 23–Nov. 21)
Triangle featured in unexpected love scenario.
Now is your chance to reach for the stars.
Unfulfilled expectations may come back to haunt
you, however. Only you can make important judg-
ment call.

TONY LASCAGLIA PRESENTED me with his birth
certificate on Wednesday morning.

Almost a week had passed since Dean and I had
made our dream date pact. Since that night I hadn't
talked to him at all. I was beginning to think he'd
given up. Maybe my perfect guy just didn't exist—
at least not within the student body of Emerald
High.

But the information on Tony LaScaglia's birth
certificate was direct evidence to the contrary. He
was born on May 5. It said so, right there in black
and white.

"What time were you born?" I asked, hardly believing I was actually having this conversation.

Tony grinned at me. I resisted the impulse to reach for my sunglasses. His teeth were so bright, they belonged in a toothpaste ad. I made a mental note to request we went somewhere dark and romantic on our date. If we didn't, I'd probably go blind.

"At nine-oh-five, Pacific daylight time. Right here in Seattle. I was born in Ballard Hospital."

"That's great," I said, trying to contain my excitement. He was my astrological soul mate! I handed the birth certificate back to him.

Tony folded it up and stuffed it in his back pocket. I stared up at him, wondering what was going to happen next.

Now that my dream date had actually revealed himself to me, I realized that Dean hadn't exactly been specific about how much he was going to tell my perfect astral match about what was going on.

"So," Tony said. "I was kind of hoping maybe we could go out. You know, since we're so perfect for each other and everything."

That answers that, I thought. Dean had obviously revealed the astrological connection. But Tony didn't seem embarrassed by it. So far, so good.

"I'd love to," I said. "What did you have in mind?"

"Something special," Tony said, easing himself onto the bench I was sitting on. He smiled again. I blinked. "Something as special as you are."

"Like what?" I asked, leaning back against his arm a little. It felt good to flirt. I hadn't done it in a long time. And it was certainly easy to flirt with

Tony. Any girl who didn't feel like flirting with him was probably dead.

"I was thinking of something romantic," Tony answered. "How does Luigi's sound?"

Luigi's was a great Italian bistro, generally regarded among the Emerald student body as being the best romantic date place in town. A guy only took a girl to Luigi's if he wanted to impress her. The occasion usually called for the guy to borrow his father's credit card.

"I don't know," I said, still flirting. "How do you think Luigi's sounds?"

"I think it's sounding better every minute," Tony answered. The five-minute warning bell rang. Our midmorning break was almost over. "So is Saturday night okay? Say about eight o'clock?"

"Sounds perfect," I said, getting up from the bench and swinging my backpack onto my shoulders. "Do you know where I live?"

"No," Tony said, another one of his smiles lighting up his features. "But I figure I've got the rest of the week to find out."

"You look great, Natalie," Jayne said.

Tonight was my big date with Tony. I was standing in front of my bedroom mirror. Jayne was sitting on my bed. She'd actually given up the possibility of a date with John to come and help me get ready. There are definite reasons why Jayne is my very best friend.

I pivoted a little in front of the mirror. "You really think that it's okay?" I said.

The dress was new. A narrow, high-waisted

white sheath with big yellow sunflowers on it. I had loved the dress at first sight. Very retro, very cool. I had even splurged and found a new pair of white, clunky-heeled shoes to go along with it.

"I think it's fabulous," Jayne said. "That brown in the center of the sunflowers really brings out the color of your eyes."

I had helped my eyes to stand out with a generous but discreet coating of mascara. But there was no sense in revealing beauty secrets if I didn't absolutely have to.

"Well, if you say so," I answered. Jayne laughed for the first time since she had arrived. I walked over and sat down next to her on the bed.

Jayne hadn't exactly fallen over herself with enthusiasm when I had told her about my date with Tony. But she hadn't tried to talk me out of it either. She did say she hoped I'd get what I wanted. Personally, I suspected my mother had been coaching her in relationship discussion lessons.

"So here I am helping you get ready for a big evening," Jayne said as I settled down beside her. "Kinda déjà vu, isn't it?"

I nodded, trying not to focus on the fact that the last time she'd helped me get ready, I had been going on a date with Dean.

I had been avoiding looking at the picture of us together as I had walked around my room getting dressed. After tonight there was a good chance I would have to put away the photograph forever. If all went well with Tony, I wouldn't have any more reason to think about Dean. The thought left a strange, hollow feeling in the pit of my stomach.

"Next time it's your turn," I told Jayne. "You and John have been together a whole week. That's longer than any of my recent relationships have lasted."

"Who'd have guessed that out of the two of us, I'd end up with the steady relationship?"

Both of us were quiet for a moment. The image of Dean's handsome face flitted before my eyes.

"Natalie," Jayne said. "I have to ask you something."

"What?" I asked, though I had a feeling I already knew what she was going to say.

"Are you sure you know what you're doing?"

"Of course I am," I said. "I'm going out with my perfect astrological match."

"Even though you don't know anything about him?" she asked.

"He's the right sign," I told her. "That's the only thing I need to know."

"But don't you think that if Tony LaScaglia were really your perfect astrological match, you would have felt some sort of Scorpio-to-Taurus spark of recognition before now?"

I had wondered the same thing myself, but now hardly seemed like the time to admit it. Instead I gave Jayne the answer I'd been giving myself all week.

"I haven't been into astrology all that long, you know. Only since I broke up with Garth. And after that, Dean distracted me."

There. I had done it. I'd said Dean's name out loud. He'd been on my mind all evening. I couldn't seem to stop wondering how Dean would be spending his night while Tony and I were out having the time of our lives.

I stood up. Thinking about Dean was only making me depressed. I couldn't focus on the past. I had to look ahead.

"Wish me luck," I said to Jayne.

Jayne stood up and gave me a hug. "Good luck, Natalie," she said. "I hope the two of you will be very happy together."

That made me laugh. "We're not getting married, Jayne. We're just going on a date."

The most important date of my life. The date that would tell me once and for all what I should trust—my instincts or my devotion to astrology.

Fourteen

DEAN

Gemini (May 21–June 20)
Snap judgments made could return to haunt you.
Are you ready for the consequences of your own actions? Only the future can decide. Bright star on
horizon could be false hope. Let your own light
shine.

"I DON'T LIKE this, Dean," John said. "This is a
very bad idea."

"You've been saying that for the last two hours," I
told him. "I don't think I need to hear it anymore."

We were huddled behind one of the busing stations at Luigi's, scraping the uneaten portions of
people's dinners off their plates.

The job would have been unappetizing enough
under normal circumstances—like, say, if we'd
been getting paid. But the reason John and I were
here was far from normal, and it didn't involve anything as simple as acquiring a paycheck.

After an entire week of telling myself I didn't have to worry about Natalie and Tony LaScaglia, I'd panicked right before their date.

The guy who owned Luigi's was an old friend of my mother's. Their friendship was part of the reason I had suggested Tony take Natalie there in the first place. I had already arranged for a special table for them.

When I'd called to beg my mom's friend to let me work at the restaurant that evening, he gave me the impression he thought I was doing industrial-strength drugs.

It had taken quite a while to convince him I was on the level. Then there was the fact that I hadn't taken any food service tests.

Finally he agreed that John and I could come down for just one night—as long as we worked a full shift, and as long as we weren't involved with anything that would put us in direct contact with food people would later be eating.

That left us dealing with what people hadn't finished, which explained why we were scraping leftovers into a bus tub. When the dishes got piled high enough, John wheeled the full cart back to the kitchen and brought us back an empty one.

Luigi's was shaped like a big crescent, which allowed for outstanding views of the water. Behind the tables was a series of freestanding walls. They were decorated to make them look like Italian frescoes. Tuxedo-clad waiters maneuvered through carefully chosen breaks in the walls.

The openings were so cleverly disguised that from the diners' side it was difficult to spot them. That fact made everything at Luigi's seem to happen as if by magic, which was part of the restaurant's charm.

The bus station where John and I were standing was behind a wall about two feet from the table where Natalie and Tony would be sitting. With luck I'd be able to overhear every word they exchanged.

The idea had seemed great when I'd come up with it in the privacy of my own bedroom. But it didn't seem so great now that I was actually putting it into effect. In fact, I felt pretty immature and childish.

"I thought this whole deal was founded on trust," John hissed as he pushed several rings of red onion off a salad plate. "When I recommended we just skip involving Tony altogether, isn't that what you said?"

"Yes, it's what I said," I hissed back, not sure how far our voices carried. "But this is different. This isn't about trust. It's about control. I have to know for myself how this turns out. That way Natalie can't surprise me anymore."

"I think you're in denial," John said, turning an empty water glass upside down. "Either you trust somebody or you don't."

"Right this way, please," I heard the maitre d' say on the other side of the divider. My hands froze above the bus tub.

"Wow, this is great," a voice said. I was sure it was Tony's.

"Pasquale will be your server," the maitre d' announced. "He will be with you in just a moment. Welcome to Luigi's. Enjoy your meal."

I think Tony and Natalie continued talking. But

I couldn't hear them over the roaring in my ears. In the next few hours my entire romantic future was going to be decided.

Either Natalie would choose me or she would choose Tony. And all I could do was to scrape dirty dishes and wait to find out which one of us it was going to be.

Fifteen

NATALIE

Scorpio (Oct. 23–Nov. 21)
Romantic cycle nearing completion. You realize
long-hoped-for dream. But unexpected events have
the power to alter situation. Analyze motivations.
Look beneath the surface. All may not be as it seems.

"WOW," TONY SAID. "A fishpond in a
restaurant. Check that out."

Together we leaned over the railing and stared at
several giant goldfish, which glided in a pond under
the bridge that led to Luigi's dining room.

"That's great," I said. "I've heard about this."

A white-jacketed maitre d' smiled at us indul-
gently. "Everyone has heard of Luigi's Lagoon," he
said. "We are famous for it. If the lady and gentle-
man would be so good as to step this way?"

So far my evening out with Tony had been absolutely fantastic. Every bit as romantic as I had hoped
it would be. He'd picked me up in his father's car—a

148

totally cool silver-and-black Mercedes. Generally speaking, I don't care what kind of car a guy drives, particularly when it's not even his. But this was supposed to be a special event. I figured it didn't hurt to appreciate top of the line.

It was true that Tony had spent the entire drive from my house to the restaurant explaining the function of each and every switch and knob on the control panel. Aside from a general "Wow, you look great" comment when he'd first seen me, he hadn't really commented on my outstanding dress. And he just didn't look at me the way Dean had when we'd gone out. There was no mysterious laughter brimming at the back of his eyes.

As Tony had pulled up in front of the entrance to Luigi's and let the attendant take the car for valet parking, I had told myself it was time to snap out of my trance. I needed to stop thinking about the past. I would concentrate solely on the events of tonight. To do any less wouldn't be fair to Tony. He deserved my full attention. After all, he was my date.

Besides, thinking only of tonight would serve one other very important function. It would mean that under absolutely no circumstances would I permit myself to think about Dean.

So far my plan seemed to be working. Tony and I had made it through the salad course. Our waiter had just whisked the plates away. A kind of peaceful lull had fallen over our table—the kind that happens when you've just experienced something great and you know something equally great is about to come.

From around the restaurant I could hear the muted conversations of the other diners. Tony looked around him, taking in the frescoed decor and the tiny strings of lights hanging from the windows.

"So," he said. "Is this a great place or what?"

I felt just the tiniest quiver of apprehension. This was about the third time that Tony had made that remark. Of course, Luigi's *was* totally great. But I was beginning to wonder if the restaurant was going to be our only topic of conversation . . . other than his father's car.

I nodded in response, just as I had the last three times Tony had said the same thing. At the rate things were going, my neck muscles were going to be sore by the end of the night.

"Absolutely," I said. "No doubt about it." I needed to change the topic of conversation. Tauruses weren't as impulsive and passionate as Scorpios were. Maybe it was up to me to establish a more intimate mood.

I leaned over the table in what I hoped was a somewhat sexy manner. "Tony, I feel like I don't really know you. Why don't you tell me what you like to do when you're not playing football."

Tony took a sip of water and considered the question. "Play baseball."

A quick clatter of plates sounded from behind one of the frescoed panels. I had to admit Tony's answer hadn't been quite what I had hoped for. He wasn't picking up at all on my playfully seductive manner. Things would have been totally different if it had been Dean.

You promised yourself you wouldn't think about him, I reminded myself. Tony's response to my question was nothing to worry about. He just had a different style.

"Baseball," I said. "That's nice."

"Oh, yeah," Tony said enthusiastically. "It's like *the* quintessential summer game."

The use of the word *quintessential* seemed somewhat promising. I didn't hear high-school jocks use that one every day.

"And so much better in hot weather than ice hockey," I said just as the waiter arrived with our entrée plates. There was another clatter of dishes from behind the panel, followed by what sounded like frantic whispering.

Tony looked at me, a frown between his eyebrows. "I'm sorry," he said. "What did you say?"

"Never mind," I said, smiling at the waiter as I mentally upped my apprehension to genuine concern. First Tony hadn't responded to how I looked. Now he wasn't responding to my jokes.

The waiter smiled back and brandished an enormous pepper mill over my fettuccine alfredo, as if it was a weapon in a kung-fu movie. "Some freshly ground black pepper for the young lady?" he asked.

"I don't think so," I said.

"And for you, sir?" the waiter said, switching direction with the pepper mill. Now it was poised and ready over Tony's plate.

I waited for Tony to glance at me across the table. Surely he'd noticed how ridiculous the routine with the pepper mill was. It would be our first private joke—the first thing we'd be totally in rapport about.

"Absolutely," Tony said, nodding enthusiastically. "Go for it."

I could feel my appetite start to vanish as

concern was replaced by genuine doubt.

Tony was a great guy. It was the one topic everybody at Emerald High agreed on. But I was beginning to wonder if the reason Tony was so popular was that there simply wasn't enough of him there to dislike. I mean, what *was* there to dislike about a guy who was as friendly as a puppy and as deep as a toddler's wading pool?

I stared at Tony across the table as he tackled his spaghetti alla carbonara. Our major topics of conversation for the evening had been football, baseball, and the fish in Luigi's Lagoon.

I was out with my perfect astrological date, and we didn't have anything to say to each other. Another few minutes of this and I'd be too bored to move.

Jayne was right about Tony and me, I thought. *There just isn't any spark of recognition between us. Worse than that. There isn't any spark at all.*

Nothing about him was funny or quirky. He didn't laugh at the same unexpected things I did. I knew Tauruses were supposed to be straight and steady. But surely my astral opposite had to have some sense of humor.

I speared a bite of fettuccine and chewed it slowly, trying to stave off a feeling of impending doom. At the rate things were going, my evening with Tony would end in total disaster. My astrological dream date would turn out to be my worst nightmare.

I'd have to confess to Dean that he had been right and I had been wrong. I shouldn't have based my decisions about our relationship on astrology. Even worse, I might even have to grovel—to ask if he still wanted to see me again.

A horrible thought occurred to me. What if Dean hadn't been completely honest when he'd said he wanted our relationship to have one last chance? Maybe this whole date with Tony was nothing but a setup. A way for Dean to get revenge.

He'd been pretty angry over what he'd thought had happened between me and Garth Hunter. What if this whole thing was nothing but a way for him to kick me while I was down?

I would admit that it had been a mistake to break up with Dean just because he was a Gemini. Then Dean would tell me to get out of his life. I'd be left with no one, and it would all be my own fault.

All of a sudden the fettuccine felt slick and slimy in the bottom of my stomach. I knew I couldn't eat another bite. "Will you excuse me, please?" I said to Tony as I pushed my chair back from the table.

"Sure," Tony said, looking up from his plate of pasta. "You look a little funny. Is everything all right?"

Now he notices how I look, I thought. *This is perfect. This is just fine.*

"I'm great," I said. "I just want to freshen up a little." I headed away from the table blindly, certain that Tony would never notice that I had just started to sound like Doris Day.

Luigi's was beautiful, but it was also incredibly confusing. I had only gone a few steps before I felt like I'd completely lost my way. The frescoed walls seemed to hem me in on all sides.

Finally I just chose a break between the frescoes. There was a busing station on the other side of the wall. It would be embarrassing, but I'd just have to ask the guys scraping dishes which way the bathroom was.

As I approached the station one of the two busboys headed toward the kitchen, pushing a cart. The other one stood motionless for a moment, with no plates to scrape.

"Excuse me," I said. "But could you please tell me—"

At the sound of my voice the busboy jerked up his head. It was Dean.

We stared at each other over the empty busing station. My whole body was tingling with pins and needles. A strange sort of ringing filled my ears.

The periodic episodes of crashing dishes suddenly made perfect sense. It hadn't just been some generic clumsy busboy. It had been a specific clumsy busboy. A busboy who had heard every word of my date with Tony.

Dean's face got very pale. I could see his Adam's apple moving up and down as he swallowed. "Natalie," he said, "I can explain. This is not what you think."

"Like you let me explain about me and Garth?" I said. My throat felt so tight, I was amazed I could speak. "Oh, please. Just spare me, Dean. You've been spying on me the whole night. You might as well admit it."

"Well, so what?" Dean said. He sounded aggressive. Obviously he was assuming that the best defense was a strong offense. "So what if I have been spying? I have a big stake in this thing."

"*This thing?* This thing happens to be my personal business," I almost shouted. "And as I recall, you promised to trust me."

"I didn't promise," Dean countered. "We never shook on it."

I could feel the blood throbbing in my temples.

154

"So," I said. "You don't trust me. You thought I'd lie about what happened between Tony and me tonight."

"No," Dean said. "I only wanted to make sure that—"

"I was telling the truth," I cut in. "Well, let me tell you something, Dean. The only time I lied was when I said I was sorry that we'd had to break up. I'm not sorry. If I had it to do over, I'd do the same thing again. Everything you've done tonight just proves my point. *You're* the one who can't be trusted. I never want to see you or speak to you again."

"Do you want to shake on *that?*" Dean said. His voice was sarcastic, but when he stuck out his hand, I noticed it was trembling. I'm not sure what I would have done if Tony hadn't appeared at exactly that moment.

"Natalie?" he called, his head popping up between the dividers. "Are you back there? What's going on?"

"Nothing's going on, Tony," I said, turning my back on Dean. I walked over to where Tony was standing, his eyes flicking back and forth between me and Dean. My back was so straight, I could have marched with the ROTC soldiers in the Fourth of July parade.

"But you know what?" I continued. "This place isn't nearly as romantic as I hoped it would be. What do you say we get out of here and go looking for some real fun?"

Tony scratched his chin, his puppy dog eyes filled with compassion. "Whatever you want, Natalie."

Sixteen

Dean

Gemini (May 21–June 20)
Disaster! Foolish actions bring harsh
consequences. Time to go home and lick
your wounds. Assess damage. Review situation.
What happens next is up to you.

"I GUESS I really blew it, didn't I?" I said as John
and I drove home from Luigi's. It was a beautiful night. Through the windshield I could see that
the sky was full of stars.

I'm sure some people would say that the sight of
stars should have made me feel much better about
the fact that I'd just been caught spying on the girl I
thought I loved. That the beauty of the night
should have made me realize how insignificant my
own problems were compared to the overall enor-
mity and glory of the cosmos.

Personally, I think that kind of thinking is
hugely overrated. Who wants to be reminded

about how unimportant they are?

I'd taken Natalie out for the first time on a night just like this. I'd kissed her under these very same stars. It didn't seem right that the night should be so beautiful now that I'd lost her forever.

"I hate to bring this up—" John began.

"Don't," I interrupted, turning down his street. "Don't say it. Things are bad enough without you saying 'I told you so.'"

"I guess you're right," John said after a minute. I maneuvered my mom's car into his drive, then killed the lights. "Do you think she saw me?" John asked, making no move to get out of the Camry.

"No," I said. "I don't think so. She was too busy being mad at me to notice anything else." I smashed my fist against the steering wheel. "How could I have been so incredibly stupid? I've lost her for good this time."

John nodded in sad agreement.

"Okay," I said. "Go ahead. Do it. I deserve it."

"I told you so," John responded quietly.

An hour later I stood under the tree in Natalie's front yard.

Her bedroom window was right above me. I could tell she was still awake because the bedroom light was on. Or maybe she wasn't even home yet. Maybe she and Tony had decided to party until dawn.

I saw a shadow pass in front of the bedroom curtain. That settled that much at least. Natalie was home. From what I could tell from down below, she was pacing around her bedroom, probably trying to calm down.

I was so wired that I didn't think I'd ever sleep again. After such a promising beginning between Natalie and me, how had things gone so wrong?

I considered searching for a handful of gravel to throw against her window. Maybe it wasn't too late. We could still talk.

Right, Dean, I thought as I watched Natalie's shadow pass by the curtains again. *And maybe she'll just pour some boiling oil down on your head.*

Natalie's shadow stopped. She was right at the center of the window. The curtains parted a little, but I couldn't tell whether or not she was looking down. More likely she was looking up, studying the alignment of the stars.

I wondered if this was how Romeo had felt when he'd waited for Juliet underneath her balcony. Except that Romeo hadn't done anything wrong. He'd thought he had his whole life ahead of him. He'd known he was going to get lucky, at least for a while. But all my luck was gone.

That's it, Dean, I thought. *You have got to get a grip on yourself. You're becoming way too morose.*

I had behaved badly. But what had gone wrong between me and Natalie wasn't all my fault. She was the one who had insisted we couldn't see each other in the first place.

Natalie stepped back from the window. A second later her bedroom light went off. I stood, leaning against the tree outside her window for at least another twenty minutes. In all that time her curtain never moved once.

She hadn't seen me, then. Or if she had, she didn't care. I got back in the car and slowly drove the short distance to my house, hoping that a good Creature Features episode would be on TV tonight. Watching a movie was the only way too kill all those empty hours before dawn.

"Dean?" my mother called as I let myself into the house. In an attempt to avoid detection I'd come in through the garage.

I should have known sneaking in wouldn't work. Mothers have built-in homing devices in case of disaster, particularly when the disaster has to do with love.

"Yeah, Mom," I said, depositing the keys on the hook near the kitchen door.

"You're awfully late. Did everything go all right at Luigi's?"

"That depends on whose side you're on."

My mother appeared in the kitchen doorway. She was wearing her hot pink chenille bathrobe and Winnie the Pooh slippers. Both had been Christmas gifts from Roy and Randy.

"I'm on your side, of course," she answered.

"Well, I hate to break this to you, but I think we lost."

"In that case you must be hungry," my mom said. "Why don't you go build us a fire to take the chill off the living room and I'll make us some hot chocolate and cinnamon toast."

"Okay," my mom said when both of us were seated in front of the fire. "Start at the beginning. Don't leave anything out."

"I was born on May 21," I said. "In a little town in—"

"Come on, Dean. Knock it off."

I lifted a piece of cinnamon toast off the plate and took a big bite.

As soon as I bit into the toast I began to feel a little better. For me, cinnamon toast therapy works every time. My mother knew this, of course. She was the one who had invented the ritual when I was little.

"So," she said, the flames from the fire reflecting off her face. "Do you want to tell me about it?"

"I screwed up, Mom. I screwed up big time."

"In what way?" she asked, taking a sip of hot chocolate.

"I set Natalie up on a date tonight, and then I hid out at Luigi's and spied on her."

My mother was quiet for a moment, taking in this information. She took another sip of hot chocolate, leaving melted marshmallow residue on her upper lip. I ate another bite of cinnamon toast.

"What? No comment?" I said, when I couldn't stand it any longer.

My mother frowned as she set down her hot chocolate. "I'm trying to think of how to answer you," she said. "You've really surprised me, Dean," she went on after a moment. "This kind of behavior doesn't sound like you at all."

"She drove me to it, Mom," I protested.

"That's a load of horse manure and you know it, Dean. What happened, honey?" she asked, her voice softening a little. "I thought you and Natalie really liked each other."

"I thought so too," I said. "But then she broke up with me for this totally stupid reason and things kind of got all fouled up."

My mother picked up her own piece of cinnamon toast. "That seems to be the understatement of the century," she said.

"Natalie thinks I spied on her because I didn't trust her. But that's really not it, Mom," I said. "I just felt like everything was happening without me and there was nothing I could do to stop it. I just wanted to take back some control."

"Oh, Dean," my mother said, abandoning her piece of cinnamon toast and looking into the fire. It had been a long time since I'd seen her look so sad. "You remind me so much of myself sometimes, honey. I made the same sort of mistake with your dad."

My mother never talks about my father. Not that she walks around being angry or hurt about what happened—she just doesn't mention him. Roy and Randy don't notice. When he walked out on us, they weren't old enough to remember him.

"You can't control love, sweetheart," my mother finally said softly. "You can't use love to make somebody do the things you want. The best you can do is to be in control of yourself. That way you have the satisfaction of knowing you've been true to your own heart, even if you don't get what you want."

"You loved Dad, didn't you?"

My mother nodded. "Of course I did, sweetheart. For a while I thought just loving him would be enough. But it takes more than one person's love to build a relationship."

"So what do I do?" I said.

My mother raised her eyebrows at me as she

reached for her cocoa. "I think you know the answer to that. You did something wrong, Dean, even if you thought you had a good reason for it."

"I have to apologize, don't I?"

"I think you do," my mother said. "But it's your decision."

"Gee, thanks a lot," I said.

My mother smiled and got up from the couch. "All this parenting has made me tired. It's time for me to go to bed. Close the fireplace screen before you turn in, honey."

"Okay," I said as she leaned over to kiss me. "Good night, Mom—and thanks."

"Don't mention it," she said. "And finish up that cinnamon toast. If Roy and Randy find out they didn't get any, I'll hear about it for a week."

I listened to her feet scuffing off toward her bedroom in her slippers. I sat and stared at the fire.

My mom was right. Somehow, between now and Monday morning, I had to find the way to tell Natalie that I was sorry. And then I had to figure out what to do with the rest of my life if she still never wanted to see me again.

Seventeen

NATALIE

Scorpio (Oct. 23–Nov. 21)
Dark night of the soul may have silver lining.
Remember that it's always darkest before the dawn.
What seems lost could be within your reach. For
way out of dilemma, try examining your own heart.

IT WAS TWO O'CLOCK in the morning, and I was still awake. Why was it that whenever all I really wanted to do was end my sorrows by falling asleep with the covers over my head, insomnia set in?

I had gotten home from my date with Tony. After leaving Luigi's we'd headed to a teen nightclub to do some dancing and blow off a little steam. Tony had been great. He had understood entirely how I felt about what had happened with Dean. He'd agreed that Dean's behavior had been totally uncalled for and outrageous. I'd actually started thinking there might be hope for us after all—right

163

up until the moment he kissed me good night under the tree in the front yard.

A girl can tell a lot about a guy from the way he kisses. I don't mean things like fancy technique. I mean things like whether or not he's actually kissing you personally or whether he just has his lips on the closest available female form.

Actually, kissing Garth should have been my first clue about what a jerk he was. I should have been able to tell right away he didn't care who I was.

Tony didn't try to maul me, but I could tell instantly that nothing serious was going to happen. Tony was just kissing a body. He wasn't kissing *me*. How could he? He hadn't really been with me all evening. We just hadn't connected.

"Thanks for everything, Tony," I said when the kiss was over. He had his arms wrapped around me to keep me warm while we stood outside beneath the tree. "It was a really nice evening."

"Uh-oh," Tony said, displaying more intuition than he had all evening. "Why do I sense a 'but' coming on here?"

"But," I said, smiling up at him. "I don't think we should see each other again."

Tony didn't say anything for a minute. "It's because of Dean, isn't it?" he asked.

"No," I answered. "It's because of you and me, Tony. You're really nice and I really like you . . . but admit it. We're wasting our time here."

Tony looked a little puzzled. Maybe he was so popular, he had never had a girl say no to him before. "You're different, aren't you, Natalie?"

"No, just brutally honest," I said. One side of

Tony's mouth quirked up. "I'd really like it if we could be friends."

"That would be great," Tony said. "Maybe you could come and watch one of my baseball games."

After Tony had left, I had done everything I could think of to stave off the inevitable: the feeling of incredible letdown. This was supposed to have been the most important evening of my life. Instead it had been my biggest fiasco.

I'd taken a long, hot bath with my favorite herbal treatment. Then I had consumed an entire pot of chamomile tea. In desperation I had even gotten out our next English assignment.

Not one distraction tactic had worked. I was actually reduced to pacing around my room. Every time I stood still, my mind instantly began replaying my entire relationship with Dean.

Even looking at the stars hadn't helped. I'd put my faith in them, and they had failed me. Worst of all, the second I opened my bedroom curtains, I could have sworn that I saw Dean. He was staring up at my window like Romeo waiting for Juliet to appear on her balcony.

I'd closed the curtains and turned off the light after that. If Dean was hanging out on my front lawn, it wasn't because he was playing Romeo to my Juliet.

Finally, totally exhausted, I had crawled into bed. I hoped that sooner or later, the fact that I was in a horizontal position would help me escape into sleep.

I'd counted sheep just to get the falling-asleep

ball rolling. Then I'd counted shepherds. Then I'd counted lambs. About the time I was seriously contemplating running through the animals on Noah's Ark, I decided the whole thing was an exercise in futility. I sat up in bed and switched on the light on my nightstand.

In the sudden brightness the first thing I saw was the picture of Dean and me at the Sweethearts' Dance. No way was I going to sit here and look at that.

I threw back the covers and scrambled out of bed. Clearly the only solution was to go downstairs and watch TV. Maybe I'd see what was on the shopping channel. QVC should put even the world's worst insomniac to sleep.

I went down to the den and turned on the television. I kept the sound down low so I wouldn't wake up my mom and dad.

Even so, my mother appeared at the doorway in less than sixty seconds. She didn't come into the den at once. That would have made it too obvious that the reason she'd gotten up was because she was worried about me. Instead she went into the kitchen. I could hear the sound of water being run into the teakettle and a plate being set on her favorite lacquer tray.

I kept my eyes on the shopping channel during all the time it took the water to boil. Finally my mother came out of the kitchen, carrying a tray with a plate of doughnuts and a pot of ginger tea.

"I felt like a midnight snack," she said as she set the tray down on the coffee table. "And I thought maybe you could use some company."

"It's two o'clock, Mom," I said. "And I couldn't possibly eat those sugar bombs in the middle of the night."

My mother handed me a plate, then a cup and saucer for my tea. "Strain yourself," she said, lifting the doughnut plate.

"If I gain ten pounds, you're paying for a whole new wardrobe," I warned her. "Which one do you think has the most chocolate on it?"

"Do you want to talk about what happened tonight?" my mother said after we'd each consumed our current weight in doughnuts and were sipping cups of fragrant ginger tea.

All those doughnuts must have weakened my resistance. I didn't even put up a fight. I told her everything, right away.

"Oh, Mom. It was so awful," I said. "Tony and I went to Luigi's for dinner, and Dean was there, spying on me."

"Spying on you?" my mother exclaimed. "Whatever for?"

"To find out what was happening between me and Tony."

My mother poured herself a fresh cup of tea. "I thought Dean arranged the date with Tony," she commented, setting the teapot back down.

"He did," I answered. "But it was really just a dare. He wanted to prove that I was being stupid about astrology. The deal was that if Tony and I went out and our evening was anything less than perfect, then I would try again with Dean."

"And how was the evening with Tony?" my

167

mother asked. "I mean, before you discovered that Dean was spying."

I folded and unfolded my napkin. "Pretty boring."

"So Dean was right," my mom said. "There wasn't any reason to pick out a date simply on the basis of astrology."

"That's not the point anymore, Mom," I protested. "Dean spied on me. He didn't wait for me to come to him and say what had happened on my date with Tony. He tried to find out for himself. He didn't trust me."

"Calm down, honey," my mother said. "I believe you. In fact, I agree. But I would like to point out that you put Dean in a pretty difficult position."

"What do you mean?"

"You broke up with Dean because of his astrological sign," she answered. "Because you were sure that as a Gemini, sooner or later Dean was going to hurt you. Am I getting this right?"

I nodded.

"So doesn't his decision to spy on you seem sort of like a self-fulfilling prophecy?"

I selected another doughnut. "I didn't set this up on purpose, Mom."

"I'm not saying that you did. But I am saying that sometimes when you believe in something strongly enough, you make it possible for your expectations to be met."

I took a sip of tea and thought this over. "Okay, I kind of see your point," I said. "But that still doesn't make what Dean did right."

"Of course it doesn't," she agreed. "What Dean did was completely lousy. And I'd be absolutely furious if anyone had done that to me. But as I see it, Dean was in a no-win situation. Nothing he did was right in your eyes, Natalie."

"Because I cared more about what sign he was than *who* he was?"

"I think that's it," my mother said.

I took another sip of tea, savoring the way the spicy ginger warmed my whole body. I put the doughnut back on the plate.

"I probably owe him some sort of apology, don't I?" I said.

My mother actually laughed. "That's about as tentative a remark as I've ever heard you make. I know it won't be easy. But I think the answer is yes. Even if you don't get back together, it would be good to clear the air between you."

"Will you come with me and hold my hand?" I asked.

"No," my mom responded. "But I'll let you practice on me if you like."

"I'm sorry if anything I did compelled you to act like an insecure and stupid jerk," I said, trying out an apology.

"You've grasped the concept, but I think your form could use a little improvement."

"I guess I'll just have to keep working on it."

I just hoped I had enough courage to go through with the real thing. . . .

"Just do it," Jayne said. "Just walk right up to him and say you're sorry."

"Will you please stop sounding like a Nike ad?"

It was Monday morning and the first day of

spring carnival. Jayne and I were putting the finishing touches on my fortune-telling booth.

In spite of the fact that I had thought about my conversation with my mother all day on Sunday, I still hadn't figured out how I was going to apologize to Dean.

The situation was making me nervous. As I saw it, we were both responsible for the horrible incident on Saturday night. If I had to apologize to him, he ought to apologize to me.

"Besides," I said. "That plan sounds kind of risky. What if he sees me coming and just walks away?"

Jayne made an irritated sound as she handed me a red silk scarf. "He won't walk away, Natalie," she said as I pinned the scarf to the canopy we'd created. "I bet he wants to say 'I'm sorry' as much as you do."

"Well, he ought to," I said.

"Oh, wonderful," Jayne said. "You're going to win him over in no time with that attitude."

We stepped away from the booth and surveyed our handiwork. Most of the carnival booths had a counter up front and room for the people working the booth in back. My fortune-telling booth was set up the other way around.

All the space was in the front so that it created a tiny room that people could step inside.

Jayne and I had stretched fabric across the top, draped scarves across the entrance, and put an old rug and some pillows on the ground. The sides of the booth were painted blue with big gold stars. I had patterned the booth after Madame Sonya's House of Fortune.

I was wearing basic black, with big hoop earrings and lots of eye makeup. I was hoping the overall effect of me and the booth together would be colorful and exotic. I wanted lots of people to wander in and pay a couple of bucks to have their fortunes told.

All the proceeds would go to junior-class special events. The whole purpose of spring carnival was for each class to raise operating funds.

"So what do you think?" I asked.

Jayne draped a blue scarf shot with gold thread on top of my head so that it fell down around my shoulders.

"I think it looks fantastic," she said. "Want me to be your first customer?"

"I already know your fortune. You're going to live happily ever after," I said.

Jayne blushed. "Free advice is always good. How about if I go scare up some customers?"

"Good idea," I said.

I crawled into the booth and settled into the corner. I arranged the pillows until I was comfortable, then tried to look mystical while I waited for the crowds. I wondered what Dean was doing. Would he make it easy for me when I tried to apologize to him? And if not, what would I do?

Dean deserved an apology, there was no two ways about it. I had to try to give him one, no matter what it took. I watched the scarves hanging from the ceiling blow in the breeze and tried not to think about whether or not Dean would be willing to give me a second chance.

The scarves at the entrance to the booth parted

and a customer came in. He was wearing black jeans and a hooded sweatshirt. The hood was pulled down across the top of his face. Between his posture and all the scarves Jayne and I had pinned to the ceiling, I couldn't quite see who my customer was.

"Welcome," I said, trying to make my voice husky and foreboding. "Have you come seeking a glimpse into what the future holds?"

The guy settled onto a clump of pillows. "Yes, I have," he said, his voice rough. It sounded like he was trying to disguise it.

Great, I thought. *My first customer and already people are playing practical jokes.*

"The past has been filled with misery," the guy said, his voice still funny. "Now I am at a crossroads."

His speech sounded kind of stilted, like he'd rehearsed it. *All right, wise guy,* I thought. "Let me see your palm," I said, holding out my hand.

He put his hand in mine, palm facing up. The life line was sure and strong. It was the kind of palm Dean would have.

"You must help me," the guy said as I continued my perusal. "I have been unlucky in love."

"Of course you have," I answered. "Have you ever heard of anyone going to a fortune-teller because they were happy in love?"

"But my situation is special," my client protested. "I have been to many fortune-tellers, trying to discover what is wrong. But no one, not even Madame Sonya herself, could help me."

Surprised, I looked up. If he had been to Madame Sonya, maybe this guy was on the level after all.

"I thought my girlfriend did not appreciate me," the guy said, his face still turned away from me. "In anger I did her a great wrong. How can I apologize so that she will believe me? How can I tell her all I want is for us to be together again?"

Tiny tremors began to radiate up my arm. This was a scenario I thought I recognized.

A gust of air blew in through the booth's entrance. The guy in front of me turned around. As he turned back I caught a glimpse of his eyes. They were smoky gray, with tiny green flecks sparkling in their depths. I could feel tears start to prick at the back of my eyes.

"Perhaps your girlfriend is also unhappy about your current situation," I said, not quite certain how I got my voice to function. "Perhaps she has realized her own mistakes and also seeks a way to make amends."

The guy's palm jerked as I held it. "Then what should I do?" he asked. "This time I have to be certain. I don't think I could take rejection again."

"She will not reject you," I promised. "You must be brave and tell her how you really feel. If you do, she will give you the answer you long for. She's not entirely stupid."

Silence filled the tent for a fraction of a second. Then the guy removed his hand from mine and pushed back the hood of his sweatshirt.

"I love you, Natalie," he whispered.

"I love you too, Dean," I said.

He reached out and pulled me to him. I think we kissed for a long time, but the world seemed to have stopped spinning while his lips were on mine.

"I'm sorry," I said when the kiss was over. "I just wanted to say that."

"I'm sorry too," Dean answered. "I can't believe I was such an incredible jerk."

"You were kind of a jerk, weren't you?" I said, smiling up at him.

"Don't press your luck, Natalie," Dean said. "Just promise me one thing."

"What?"

"That you'll chill on this astrology business."

"I promise," I whispered. "On one condition."

Dean's eyebrows went up. The green flecks in his eyes were dancing. "And that is?"

"That we abandon the fortune-telling business and you let me pay a dollar for you to take four chances to soak Garth Hunter at the dunking booth."

Dean's smile was brighter than any star in the heavens. "Done."

"Let's shake on it," I said.

Eighteen

NATALIE

Scorpio (Oct. 23–Nov. 21)
Perfect planet alignment highlights personal
victory, reunion with one you love. What seemed
impossible to resolve now has happy outcome.
All's well that ends well.

"IT'S NICE TO finally meet you, Natalie," Dean's
mom said.

"Thanks, Mrs. Smith," I answered. "It's nice to
meet you too."

Spring carnival was over. Dean had insisted we
commemorate the fact that we were back together
again by taking me to meet his mom and little
brothers after school. He seemed to want to get the
only other potential obstacle to our happiness out
of the way as soon as possible.

I told him his little brothers couldn't possibly be that
bad. He told me I should wait until I'd had a chance to
meet them before I made any snap judgments.

Jayne and John had tagged along with us for positive reinforcement. We'd been hanging out all afternoon.

It was the first time all four of us had spent time together as official couples. Dean had kicked off the celebration of our being back together by hitting four out of four bull's-eyes to plunge Garth Hunter into the icy water at the dunking booth.

"A carnival," Dean's mom said now as she passed around a plate of cookies. Roy, or maybe it was Randy, took the biggest one, hopped down from his chair, and raced for the backyard.

"I'm not eating with Dean and his girlfriend. What if he kisses her? It's gross," he yelled.

"Triple gross," the other twin added, grabbing his own cookie and following close behind.

"You'll have to excuse the boys," Dean's mother told me, shaking her head sadly. "I'm afraid they're not quite housebroken."

I took a cookie and handed the plate to Jayne. "As I was saying," Dean's mother continued. "I went to a carnival the day Dean was born. We were living in Miami then. My husband was on his first freelance journalism assignment."

"Wait a minute," I said, my cookie poised halfway to my mouth. "You mean Dean was born on East Coast time?"

"Natalie," Dean said. "You promised." I ignored him.

"Yep," his mother answered. "Almost exactly at midnight. I had a discussion with the doctor about which day he was really born on."

I set my cookie down on the table. I could

hardly believe it. Dean had been born at midnight between May 20 and May 21. On East Coast time.

My instincts had been right. And so had my devotion to astrology. The three-hour time difference changed everything. Dean was a Taurus after all.

And the fact that he'd been born on the cusp explained so much about his nature. It explained his steadiness. The fact that he hadn't given up on me in spite of impossible odds. Those things were straight Taurus. But the Gemini portion of his makeup accounted for his zany sense of humor and the way he always wanted to turn everything into a dare.

"Natalie?" Dean asked. "Do you feel all right?"

"I feel fine," I answered, reaching out my hand. I wrapped my fingers around his. They fit together perfectly. "Everything is fine."

I wouldn't tell him that he was really a Taurus yet. We had just worked things out between us. There was no need to complicate matters by telling him I'd been wrong—and right—about him all along.

There's no rush, I thought as I squeezed Dean's fingers. Out of the corner of my eye I saw his mother smile.

There would be plenty of time to explain things to him. Dean and I were going to be together for a long time. We had to be. We were made for each other.

And now I knew for certain that our love was written in the stars.

LOVE STORIES ASTROLOGICAL LOVE GUIDE

Do you believe your fate is written in the stars? Are you destined to be together like Gwyneth and Brad? Superman and Lois Lane? Romeo and Juliet? Well, okay, that last one's a pretty dismal example. But before you go jumping into a star-crossed relationship like theirs, read Jenny's astrological love guide. Avoid a catastrophic confrontation with destiny.

ARIES: *(March 21-April 19)*
"I know exactly what I'm doing," is your catchphrase. With great spirit and faith, you dive into relationships headfirst, throwing caution to the wind. But however devoted you may be in the beginning, your yawn fest starts

early. Boredom is one thing an action-seeking Aries can't handle! A quick-witted **GEMINI** will keep you laughing with his sharp sense of humor, but more importantly, he'll keep you interested. Steer clear of the **TAURUS** guy. He will not put up with your need to always be right.

TAURUS: (April 20–May 20)

Like a stoic medieval heroine, you live your life with strength and courage. Loyal to the end, a Taurus is trustworthy and majorly into commitment. Find a strong and responsible **CAPRICORN,** and he'll revel in your nurturing spirit while remaining true only to you. When it comes to **GEMINI,** don't even go there! He thrives on change and lives in the now, while you crave stability and security.

GEMINI: (May 21–June 20)

You're always at the center of the party— your buds are in awe of your effortless flirting techniques. You love to be out and about and want a guy who can show you a great time. A charming, excitement-seeking **SAGITTARIUS** is the perfect match for you. Together you'll dance the night away.

But stay away from any guy who wants to tie you down, like homebody **TAURUS**.

CANCER: *(June 21-July 22)*

Sensitive and caring, you're a supportive friend and a caring girlfriend. Just watch out for a tendency to mother your guy—accept the fact that he actually *likes* eating pork rinds for breakfast. A thoughtful, poetic **PISCES** guy would be lucky to have you, but don't get sucked in by charming **SAGITTARIANS** who notice your kindness just long enough to take advantage of it before they're out of there.

LEO: *(July 23-August 22)*

Girlfriend, you need a guy who'll treat you like a queen—you want to be romanced in high style. Everything your way is the only way for you. But you give as good as you get, and once a guy proves himself to you, you're in it for the long haul. A fellow **LEO** is your best love match; he intuitively understands how you want to be treated. Wet-blanket **VIRGOS** will only try to put out your fabulous fire.

VIRGO: *(August 23-September 22)*

Even as you're recording every minor

appointment in your datebook, you're secretly longing to be romantically swept away. Caring, helpful, and compulsively organized, your perfect mate is another **VIRGO**. Only he can understand your need to color code your sock drawer. Stay away from the selfish **ARIES** man. Breaking dates and destroying your routine, he'll leave you shattered and alone to pick up the pieces.

LIBRA: *(September 23-October 22)*

Sophisticated Libras crave romance in the form of candlelight, long-stemmed roses, and fine crystal. Find a guy who's as elegant and mature as you are, and you've met your match in another dreamy-eyed **LIBRA**. From here on in it's love, romance, and lots of cuddling. If an immature **SAGITTARIUS** comes your way, give him a lollipop and say "Thanks, but no thanks." He's no match for your sophistication.

SCORPIO: *(October 23-November 21)*

You are intensely emotional and full of passion, but you're careful to mask your feelings. The nurturing and intuitive **CANCER** guy is your perfect match. He sees through your protective armor and is tuned in to your every mood swing. Don't hook up with a flighty **GEMINI**. He won't sit still long enough to give you the support and attention you crave.

SAGITTARIUS: (November 22-December 21)

Socially, you're a chameleon who's comfortable in any situation and thrives on new experiences. The lazy **TAURUS** guy is your worst nightmare. Leave him snoring on the couch and head for a **GEMINI**. This ball of energy will take you white-water rafting, ballroom dancing, or hiking in search of the perfect picnic spot. Your biggest challenge as a couple will be deciding which uncharted waters to explore next.

CAPRICORN: (December 22-January 19)

Energetic, dependable, and nurturing, your only fault is not believing in your own worth. The realistic and straightforward **VIRGO** guy will bring you up when you're down by stating the obvious—it doesn't get any better than you! Avoid the nonchalant **SAGITTARIUS**. When you want to talk about something that's important to you, he'll get uncomfortable and blow it off as "no big deal."

AQUARIUS: *(January 20-February 18)*

Because you are inquisitive, peppy, and eternally friendly, you thrive in groups and in friendships more than in one-on-one relationships. Show a flighty and attention-seeking **LIBRA** just how loving you are and he won't know what hit him. He's never felt so intense about anyone, making for a deep and exciting relationship. A quiet **CANCER** who always wants you alone will only cramp your style.

PISCES: *(February 19-March 20)*

Sensitive and thoughtful, you're drawn toward the musical, artistic type of guy who needs your superempathetic spirit. Find a romantic, starry-eyed **CANCER** and you're in for long walks on the beach, tons of flowers, and undying devotion. A self-absorbed **LEO** will not be sensitive to your feelings and will only turn you into a whining lump of mush.

Happy hunting! Love, Jenny

Note from Jake: Just so you know, I would like to disassociate myself with this entire column. I don't subscribe to any of this "fate" insanity and my romantic life has always been quite satisfying, thank you very much!

Love, Jake

Do you ever wonder about falling in love? About members of the opposite sex? Do you need a little friendly advice but have no one to turn to? Well, that's where we come in . . . Jenny and Jake. Send us those questions you're dying to ask, and we'll give you the straight scoop on life and love in the nineties.

DEAR JAKE

Q: *My boyfriend, Kevin, freaked out on me the other day and I don't know what to do. We have been together for a really long time so we've obviously argued before. But in the past, when we've fought, it's been a kind of civilized fighting—if that's possible. We always listened to each other and we had a mutual promise never to say anything really hurtful.*

But the during this last argument, he got personal and extremely mean. I told him I was hurt by a comment he had made about my appearance and he just flew off the handle. He was screaming at me so much I was actually afraid of him. The thing is, I didn't do any-thing wrong. I called him on something he did to hurt me and he lost it. His dad has an irrational temper but Kevin has never acted like this before. Do you think he's turning into his father?

SB, Houston, TX

A: It is possible for temper to run in a family. You don't want to be around when my uncles get into a football "conversation" over Thanksgiving dinner.

But my brother and I don't seem to have bad tempers, so it's not a given thing. After just one outburst I wouldn't worry.

The question is, did he apologize? He must know he was wrong; only the extremely thick-headed don't realize when they hurt a girl as badly as Kevin hurt you. If he's brave enough, and sensitive enough to your feelings to apologize, that's a step in the right direction. Next time he'll think about it before he yells at you.

If he didn't apologize, you should talk to him about what happened. Maybe he'll be able to have a civil conversation about it, like you two normally do. Tell him you were scared—that will really open his eyes. If he gets angry at you again, it's time to reevaluate your relationship. If he's not paying attention to your feelings anymore, and he can't get over your argument, he's not worth it.

DEAR JENNY

Q: *My ex-boyfriend, Matt, and I went out for four months, and we recently broke up. Now, for no apparent reason, he's spreading rumors about me. He's telling all the guys that he'll beat them up if they ask me out and he's turning everybody against me.*

There's one guy, Kenneth, who I really like. I thought he liked me too, but now he's listening to Matt. Matt's a little old to be playing these games but I don't know how to make him see that. He's ruining my life! How do I get him to stop talking about me?

JM, Kend, IN

A: Unfortunately, this kind of thing happens all the time when couples break up. Matt is just being immature because he doesn't know how to handle not being with you. He's confused and he's focusing his energies on bringing you down because he wants you to be as upset as he is.

Honestly, the best thing to do in this situation is to ignore it. I know it sounds hard, but if you don't let him see he's having an affect on you, he'll give up. It's amazing how quickly people forget about these rumors and threats. Some other scandal will come along for them to talk about and things will go back to normal.

In the meantime, try to talk to Kenneth. Let him know that none of this stuff that Matt is saying is true. If he likes you, maybe he'll see that Matt is a liar and take your side. Wouldn't that be worth the effort of getting up the courage to call him?

Do you have questions about love? Write to:

Jenny Burgess or Jake Korman
c/o Daniel Weiss Associates
33 West 17th Street
New York, NY 10011